AN EXPLOSIVE BUSINESS

Alice Greene walked to her car with long steps. She got into the Mercedes, and with the light on from the open front door, the two men in the doorway could see her fumbling in her purse for her car keys.

"Sy," Masuto said, "get into your car and follow her. Anything—even a rolling stop at a stop sign—anything. The moment she steps out of line, pull her in for drunk driving."

At that moment, just as Beckman took off for his car, Alice slammed her car door, switched on her lights, and turned the ignition key.

The explosion rocked the house and the burst of flame lit up the driveway.

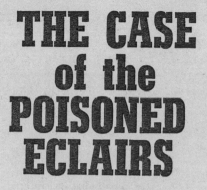

THE CASE
of the
POISONED
ECLAIRS

E. V. Cunningham

A DELL BOOK

To the memory of Louis Untermeyer

Published by
Dell Publishing Co., Inc.
1 Dag Hammarskjold Plaza
New York, New York 10017

Published by special arrangement with Eric Lasher.

Dell ® TM 681510, Dell Publishing Co., Inc.

ISBN: 0-440-11256-7

Reprinted by arrangement with Holt, Rinehart and Winston.

Printed in the United States of America

First Dell printing—October 1980

Chapter 1

SAM BAXTER

Masao Masuto was late at his morning meditation. Here it was already a few minutes past eight o'clock in the morning and still he sat cross-legged, like a saffron-robed Buddha, in the little sunparlor which he was pleased to call his meditation room. Kati, his wife, sent the two children off to school in a flurry of whispers, and then she stood staring at the figure of her husband. Had he fallen asleep? That, she knew, would be the ultimate sin in meditation—provided there was such a thing as a sin in meditation. She herself did not meditate; it was quite enough, she once told her husband, to run the house and take care of the children—aside from which she felt no need. She was not a policeman, thank heavens; her husband was.

She was in the kitchen, putting his breakfast together, when she heard him rise and go into the bedroom to dress. A few minutes later he leaned over her and kissed the spot where her neck joined her shoulder.

"That does not make everything all right," she said.

"Is everything not all right?"

"I have been reading an article by Betty Friedan. About women. Do you know what she says about Japanese women?"

"Ah so. Will I get my breakfast or must I eat at the hash joint?"

"Your breakfast is already on the table."

"You are really the most wonderful of wives," Masuto told her.

"Only because I never stand up for my rights. Sono Asie is starting a consciousness-raising group for Nisei women. She asked me to join."

"Are you asking me or telling me?"

"I'm not sure."

"It's an excellent idea," Masuto said.

"You agree?"

"Why not? Higher consciousness is excellent in any situation, and if you neglect my home and my children, I can always divorce you and find a truly submissive woman."

"Why must you always tease me?"

"Tease you? Never." He finished eating, rose, and put his arms around her. "I love you very much. Join any group you wish. Now I must go."

"To violence and death and murder. And now I have another day of worry."

"Absolutely not," Masuto said cheerfully. "There has been no death by violence in Beverly Hills for five weeks. In fact, I should not be surprised if they closed down the homicide department. Then I should be an ordinary policeman admonishing children of the rich who sniff cocaine and lecturing housewives on how to keep their oversized houses from being burgled."

"That would not make me unhappy," Kati told him.

Would it make him unhappy? As he drove north on Motor Avenue from Culver City, where he lived, into Beverly Hills, Masuto wondered about that. He had been in charge of Beverly Hills' tiny homicide squad for five years now. Could it be that he had become fascinated with murder? It was the ultimate crime, the single hideous mark of the beast that had scarred man since Cain first raised his hand against his brother Abel. Of course, that was a Western myth; yet Masuto, like most Nisei, was a man whose consciousness was split between East and West.

"Why do men murder?" Kati had once asked him.

"Because they lose themselves somewhere," he had replied, "and in that way they lose the rest of mankind."

"That is a Zen answer," Kati said with irritation. "You only confuse me with your Zen answers."

He reached the police station on Rexford Drive, parked, and went upstairs. Well, he confused Kati, and very often he confused himself; there was no easy answer when he asked himself why he was a policeman—any more than an easy answer to the question of why murder was done. Yet he was content to remain where he was, to accept the fact that promotion was unlikely, that Beverly Hills was not yet ready for a Nisei chief of police. He had all that he desired, a good wife, two children, his meditation, and his rose garden.

In his office, Sy Beckman, the other half of the homicide division, was at his desk, feet up, reading the Los Angeles *Times*. "Quiet day," he said to Masuto. "In L.A., on the other hand, they got five homicides."

"I don't envy them."

"Wainwright says to find him as soon as you come in."

Wainwright—Captain Wainwright of the Beverly Hills Police Department—sat behind his desk and stared sourly at Masuto. His expression indicated nothing; it had become fixed many years before, and Masuto could remember and count the times he had smiled. "Over at All Saints," he said to Masuto, "Doc Baxter has a cadaver that he wants you to look at. Anyway, it's time you and Beckman stirred your asses and justified my having a homicide division."

"We haven't been sitting still," Masuto said gently. "We've been on robbery. However, if the city fathers require murder, we can hire a contract man—"

"Oh, get the hell out of here," Wainwright said tiredly. "Your humor stinks."

"Do you want me?" Beckman asked Masuto.

"Finish the paper. It's just possible I can handle Baxter alone."

"Funny."

Beverly Hills, in spite of the astonishing growth of the small, affluent city that was entirely surrounded by the city of Los Angeles, was still too small to have its own morgue and department of forensic medicine. Instead, it used the morgue and pathology room at All Saints Hospital, which was located just at the edge of Beverly Hills, one small wing extending into the domain of Los Angeles. Dr. Sam Baxter was part-time medical examiner for Beverly Hills, a tired, professionally nasty internist in his late sixties. He regarded each summons to work as a deliberate intrusion on his time and privacy, whereby he specificed the members of the Beverly Hills police force as his nominal enemies.

He greeted Masuto with a cold stare. "Do you know how long I been waiting here? It's almost ten."

"I was informed and I came immediately," Masuto said gently.

"What the hell, I'm not a cop. Or am I? Tell me?"

"No, doc. You're not a cop."

"But I got to turn up murder. God knows how many killers are walking the streets because you lamebrains over there on Rexford Drive can't see what's in front of your noses."

"We do our best."

"I just bet you do."

"What have you got?" Masuto asked him. "Mostly we're told about murder. It's still sort of a novelty in Beverly Hills."

"Don't get snotty with me, Masao. You're the chief of what they please to call their homicide squad, heaven help us." As he talked, he walked across the hospital morgue to the refrigerated holding cabinet and pulled out one of the drawers. "Take a look at this."

Masuto walked over to the cabinet and looked down at the pale, lifeless face of a young woman. Her hair was black, her features good. In death, she was wistful, as if pleading for all the years of life that had been taken from her.

"Ana Fortez," Baxter said. "Twenty-one years old. Admitted to All Saints the night before last with a severe case of food poisoning. Died yesterday afternoon. Botulism."

Masuto nodded. "We had a report."

"I don't doubt it. Did the report tell you that in the eight hours before she had been taken ill she had eaten three chocolate éclairs and nothing else?"

"I think that was mentioned."

"You think so," Baxter said sarcastically. "You really think so. And then she died. But you defenders of law and order saw nothing unusual in that—nothing unusual in botulism from eating a chocolate éclair?"

"Look, Doc, I appreciate your wit and irony. We

were waiting for your autopsy report, out of due respect for our medical examiner. People do die from food poisoning."

"Not from éclairs."

"Why not from éclairs? The scouts have a picnic. Someone brings creampuffs, and thirty scouts end up in the hospital. It's happened time and again."

"But they don't die, mister—not from a botulism."

"Why not? I seem to remember fatalities."

"No, sir. Not from botulism. There are a dozen other kinds of food poisoning, but botulism is the rattlesnake of the lot and it does not grow in éclairs. It grows in putrefying meat and in badly canned vegetables. Did you ever pick up a can and find both ends bloated? Throw it away. It could contain a botulin. The bacillus botulinus will grow only in the absence of air, and there's no such thing as an airtight éclair, and this poor kid had enough botulin in her stomach to kill a horse. From eating éclairs? Now you tell me how the botulin got into the éclairs?"

"She's a Chicano?"

"I suppose so."

"Maybe she ate a bad taco. The meat some of those places use—"

"Shrewd, shrewd," Baxter agreed. "The cops are getting wiser. Why didn't I find it in her stomach?" He pushed the drawer back into the holding cabinet. "Tell you something, Masuto, if I had to choose between being bitten by a rattlesnake and swallowing botulin, I'd take the rattlesnake hands down."

"Is it always fatal?"

"Just about. The toxin does it—intoxication, we call it—" he grinned. "That's the medical term."

"All right," Masuto said, "you've been very clever and I salute you. Now what are you telling me? Are you telling me that this poor kid was murdered deliberately by someone injecting a batch of éclairs with botulin and then feeding them to her?"

"That's right. That's just what I'm telling you."

"It's the most far-fetched thing I ever heard of."

"I don't perpetrate the murders, Sergeant, I just analyze them."

"Are you sure?"

"You're damn right I'm sure."

"Was the kid married? Does she have a husband, family, friends?"

"That's upstairs business. I just open them up."

The hospital records listed her husband, Pedro Fortez, as next of kin. Masuto copied down the address—an East Los Angeles street—and the phone number, informed the hospital that the death had become a police matter, and then returned to the headquarters.

"Pretty damn unlikely," Captain Wainwright said after Masuto had filled him in. "Who is the kid?"

"A Chicano, occupation housemaid."

"And someone puts together this crazy murder device? Balls! You know what I think? I think Doc Baxter has flipped out."

"He only does the autopsy. It's the pathologist at the hospital who came up with the botulism."

"Then we'll find the goddamn bakery and close it down. I don't buy that crap that an éclair can't kill you. My wife ate a rotten éclair once and she was in the hospital three days. Meanwhile, get through to L.A.P.D. and see if they got any cases of food poisoning. Check the County Health Service too."

Masuto nodded slowly.

"You don't agree with me," Wainwright said. "You got one of those Chinese hunches of yours."

"I don't know. Anyway, I have to talk to her husband. He's my only lead to the bakery."

"Talk to him. Only don't go looking for trouble, Masao. It finds us soon enough."

In Masuto's office, Beckman had finished the Los Angeles *Times* and was reading the *Herald-Examiner*.

"Perhaps I should wait until you finish the paper," Masuto suggested.

"Just trying to catch up. You don't read the papers, you're not in the world."

"I'm returning you to the world. Go downtown and talk to Omi Saiku. He runs the poison lab for the Los Angeles cops. He's a fourth or fifth cousin of mine, so you can tell him that you're asking for me."

"What am I asking him?"

"You're asking what he has on recent food poisoning in general, and specifically whether a bad éclair can produce botulism."

"How do you spell botulism?"

Masuto spelled it out. "And get a background. If he tells you no botulism in an éclair, find out if someone could put it there. Find out if a person eating it could taste it. Get all the background you can, and then go to the County Health Service and see what they have on recent food poisoning."

"You don't think you ought to fill me in?"

"I don't know what's to fill in yet. Baxter has a Chicano girl over at All Saints who he claims was murdered by éclairs doped with botulin. It sounds crazy."

"You can say that again," Beckman agreed.

After Beckman had left, Masuto called the telephone number the hospital had given him. A voice answered in Spanish. Speaking careful, well-enunciated Spanish, Masuto asked for Pedro Fortez and was told that he was at All Saints Hospital.

Masuto drove back to All Saints, and as he entered the lobby, he noticed sitting on one of the benches a young man whose face reflected all the grief a face could hold, a dark, good-looking young man of about thirty. Masuto walked over to him and asked, speaking Spanish, "Are you Pedro Fortez?"

The eyes, wet with tears, looked at Masuto. The head nodded.

"I am Sergeant Masuto, Beverly Hills police. I hesitate to intrude on your grief, but I must talk to you. I must ask you some questions."

Fortez nodded mutely.

"We can speak in Spanish or English, whichever is easier for you. Spanish?"

"Sí," the young man whispered.

"Your wife was employed as a domestic?"

"She worked for Mrs. Crombie."

"You know the address?"

He gave an address on Beverly Drive, and Masuto jotted it down. "Can you tell me," Masuto asked gently, "what happened the day your wife took sick?"

There was a long silence. Then Fortez drew a long breath and said, "Nothing happened. That's what is so terrible. We have one car, my old Ford. I work in a plastics plant in Santa Monica. When I go to work in the morning, I drop Ana off at the Crombie place. In the evening, I pick her up—only—"

The tears began again. The nurse at the reception desk came over and whispered to Masuto. Was there something she could do? "Poor kid," she said. "Are you a friend?"

"I'm a policeman," Masuto said. "Perhaps a little water."

Fortez drank the water and apologized for his tears. "We were only married a year," he explained.

"And you picked Ana up the night before last?"

"Yes. We drove home. She had a dish in the refrigerator that she had prepared for me the night before. It is called *carne de res con nopalitos* and it is made with much garlic and green cactus. Ana could not bear the taste of garlic. She made the dish just for me. I asked her what she would eat, and she showed me the three éclairs that Mrs. Crombie let her take home. My Ana was like a little child about sweets. She decided that the pastry would be her whole supper."

"She didn't offer you any?"

He shook his head. "I don't like such things."

"And after she ate the pastry, she became sick?"

"That night she became sick. In the morning I called the ambulance. It was too late. Then when she died—when she died—they brought her body here."

"Do you know why they brought her body here, Mr. Fortez?"

"They said she was poisoned, that the food poisoned her."

"Yes. Your wife died of a kind of food poisoning called botulism. That's what makes it a police matter. You see, we must try to find out where the éclairs came from. I don't know whether there is any reason why you must stay here now. Could you leave and return?"

He nodded.

"We would be very grateful to you if you could come to the Beverly Hills police headquarters and give us a statement. I only mean to let a stenographer take down what you have just told me. Then you could sign it, and we have it for the records."

"Must I? Ana is here. I arranged for the hearse to come here for her body."

"When?"

"At three o'clock."

"Then you have plenty of time. This won't take more than an hour, with the driving. I'll be happy to drive you both ways."

He thought about it for a while, then nodded. "I'll take my own car."

"The police station is on Rexford, just south of Santa Monica. Do you know where that is?"

"I know. Yes."

After Fortez had made his statement, and after it was typed up and Wainwright had read it, the captain said to Masuto, "Did you tell him about Doc Baxter's theory?"

"No. What for? He has enough grief."

"Still, if there's anything to it, he could have fed her the stuff in a mug of coffee."

"Come on," Masuto said. "A Mexican murder is an act of violence, an act of rage. If this is what Baxter says it is, it's a thousand years removed from those poor kids. It's diabolical."

"If it's what Baxter says it is. I still don't buy it."

Beckman walked in as Masuto entered his office, and stood in silence for a long moment, watching Masuto.

"What is it, Sy? What did you learn?"

"You give me a creepy feeling at times."

"That's because I'm a wily Oriental. What did Omi have to say?"

"He says you can't get botulism from an éclair. He also says you can't get botulism from Lubie's chocolates, which in case you never heard of Lubie's chocolates are maybe the most expensive candy in the world, and they're sold on North Cañon Drive over here in Beverly Hills for eight and a half dollars a pound."

"I know the place where they sell Lubie's chocolates."

"On your pay?"

"I don't buy them. I just know where they're sold. So maybe you'll be good enough to tell me what the devil you're talking about."

"All right. All right." Beckman spread his hands. "Other cops, they got muggers and rapists. We got the cutes, only not so cute. I go downtown and ask all the questions. Absolutely quiet on the food poisoning front, not even a troop of boy scouts who let their sandwiches sit in the sun too long, not even a restaurant closed down for a dirty kitchen, except—"

"Except what?"

"This cousin Omi Saiku of yours, strange duck, knows more about poison than an encyclopedia, shows me some sweet pea seeds—deadly. You ever know that? You can die from eating sweet pea seeds or morning glory seeds or potato leaves—"

"Will you please get to the point? What about Lubie's chocolates?"

"I'm getting there. I'm just saying I'm glad he's on our side. So he says to me, 'Masao's found a botulin in an éclair.' Then he grins, like it's some special earth-shaking discovery in the poison field. 'Then tell Masao we found a botulin in a chocolate bonbon. He will enjoy that. I am sure that police work in Beverly Hills is very dull.' Then he tells me that this dame—" He took out his notebook to consult it. "Name of Alice Greene, lives over here on Roxbury Drive. Well, he tells me that she feeds a couple of pieces of this Lubie candy to her dog, a Pekinese, and the dog freaks out. She takes the dog to her vet over on Western, a Dr. Carver, but he can't save the dog. However this Dr. Carver is no fool and he gets this Greene lady to go back and bring him the candy. Then he sends the candy along to Cousin Omi, and what do you think?"

"The candy is loaded with botulin."

"Right. The whole top layer, nine of these oversized chocolate creams. This cousin Omi of yours, he says that if the candy produced the botulin, it's the first time in either the history of candy or botulism that it happened. Only it didn't happen. Omi shows me exactly how the stuff was shot into the candy pieces, as crazy as that sounds. Can you imagine feeding eight-and-a-half-dollar candy to a mutt?"

"It wasn't meant for a dog. What the devil do we have here? Omi gave you the candy, didn't he?"

"No. He wants to run some more tests. He knows we don't have a poison lab, and anyway he wants to talk to you. He says you should come down there first chance you get."

"What about prints?"

"They took care of that and Dr. Carver was careful. The only prints on the box are Mrs. Greene's. That's as far as they're taking it down at the Los Angeles cops. They say it's our turf and our case."

"I hope you thanked them," Masuto said bleakly.

Chapter 2

LAURA CROMBIE

"I swear to God," Captain Wainwright said, "I've lost my taste for this lunatic world we live in. Snipers sit up on the hillsides and shoot motorists they've never met, terrorists execute heads of state, and lunatics poison Pekinese dogs."

"All killers are lunatics, to one degree or another," Masuto said. "This one is sick, very sick."

"Well, at least you got something to work with. Someone brought the éclairs and someone bought the candy. Run that down and we have our man," Wainwright said.

"Perhaps."

"And keep it quiet, Masao. If there's one thing this city doesn't need, it's a bizarre murder case."

"I'll keep it as quiet as I can, but nothing's going to wash out the fact that it's bizarre. That's exactly what it is," Masuto responded.

Beckman agreed with Masuto. "When I was with the L.A. cops, Masao," he said, "a killing was done with a knife or a gun. But this botulism—"

"All right, but it's our baby now, so you get over to the people at Lubie's Sweet Shop and try to jog their memories. They're going to put you off and tell you that they sell a hundred boxes of that stuff every day, but I don't think they do, even in Beverly Hills. Was it a one-pound box?" Wainwright asked Beckman.

"It was," Beckman answered.

"Did you note the arrangement of the candy, the color, the shapes?" Masuto asked.

"Was I born yesterday, Masao?"

"Then give them the information as precisely as possible and just keep working at them until they remember something," Masuto said.

"I'll do my best."

"Then meet me at the Crombie place. It's on Beverly Drive. Better jot down the address."

The Crombie house wasn't large, considering its location on Beverly Drive in the very center of Beverly Hills. The tourist buses, which can be seen at almost any time of any day twisting up and down the streets of Beverly Hills, never failed to include Beverly Drive between Santa Monica Boulevard and Sunset Boulevard. This stretch of about a mile of glamorous homes had once housed some of the most glittering film stars of another age. The stars had died or moved away, but the houses remained, and the Crombie house was by no means the grandest among them. Architecturally, it would have been called a modified French château, and since it was large enough for six or seven bedrooms, Masuto was somewhat surprised that the woman who opened the door for him stated that she was Mrs. Laura Crombie.

She was a tall, handsome woman in her mid-forties, with a lean body, a well-defined face, light-brown hair swept back from her brow, and little makeup. She wore slacks and a blouse, and regarded Masuto curiously from behind the chain which held the door half open.

"I'm Detective Sergeant Masuto, Beverly Hills police," he said, showing her his badge. "I'd like to talk to you, if you don't mind."

"Yes—yes, of course. Is it about Ana, poor child? I called the hospital, and they told me." She unhooked the chain. "Forgive me, but I'm alone in the house. I've had no one to replace Ana." She stood aside for him to enter, closing the door behind him. "You're Japanese. Forgive me. I don't usually make personal remarks. I think it's fine that we have a Japanese policeman here."

"I'm a Nisei, Mrs. Crombie, which means I was born here. However, you may think of me as Japanese if you wish. I am not entirely Westernized."

"You're very nice, and that's a very nice way to forgive my rudeness. Come in and sit down. Can I offer you anything, a cold drink, perhaps?"

"No, thank you, nothing."

She led the way through a living room furnished with overstuffed pieces covered in bright printed linen into a library, bookshelves and brown leather chairs and couch. All in good taste, Masuto reflected, a huge and enormously expensive Kirman rug on the floor of the living room and three lovely Degas pastels on the wall of the library. She sat down in one of the leather chairs, and he sat facing her.

"I will have to ask you a good many questions," he told her. "I hope you will not mind and I hope you can give me the time."

"No—I don't mind and I do have the time. But why?" she wondered, frowning. "I think Ana's death is a terrible thing—she was so young and alive and bright. But food poisoning happens, and I've begged her not to eat those wretched tacos."

"She didn't die from eating tacos or any other Mexican food, Mrs. Crombie. She was poisoned by the éclairs you gave her to take home."

There was a long silence. Then Mrs. Crombie whispered, "Oh, my God, no. No!"

"I'm afraid so."

The woman sitting across from Masuto shook her head woefully. "Oh, I'm sorry. I'm so sorry."

"It wasn't your fault. I know how you must feel," he said gently.

"Of course it was my fault, I gave her the pastry."

"There was no way you could have known what you were giving her. Did you eat any of the pastry or did you give her all of it?"

Laura Crombie shook her head, tried to speak, then closed her eyes.

"Can I get you something?" Masuto asked her.

"No—give me a minute. I'll be all right." A moment later, she appeared to have recovered. "Go on, Sergeant."

"The important thing is to know where you bought the pastry."

"I didn't buy it."

"You didn't buy it? Was it a gift? Did someone bring it?"

"It was delivered."

"But who sent it? Who brought it?"

She shook her head. "You must think me a totally empty-headed fool. I'll try to explain. I am divorced, and I live alone in this huge, ridiculous barn of a place. I don't know why. Inertia, and also some good memories as well as some bad ones. Ana took care of the place. I don't entertain very much. I don't go out much and I dislike travel intensely. I have all the money I could possibly need and I find myself bored to distraction. Years ago, I used to play bridge. Last month, I decided to try to put a bridge game together, which would take care of at least one afternoon a week. I had two friends who were interested, and then we found a third. The day before yesterday was the third afternoon we met. I always serve something—tea, sandwiches, fruit, sometimes salad. But all four of us watch our weight fanatically. That's the Beverly Hills syndrome, you know. Well, just before my friends arrived—that was about noon—the pastry was delivered. I was sure it was from one of them, but they all denied it. You know—big joke, conversation piece, let's forget about calories for once in our lives and take the plunge—how much can you gain from one éclair? Then it turned into a sort of contest of will power, and in the end, not one of us touched the stuff. Then when Ana, poor child, was ready to leave, she saw me start to throw the pastry into the garbage pail. She said, I think, 'Oh, no please, not those beautiful éclairs!' So I gave her the éclairs. How could I refuse her?"

"No, you couldn't," Masuto agreed. "That was all—three éclairs?"

"Oh, no. There were eight pieces, if I remember right. Three éclairs, three strawberry tarts, and two feuilletés à la crème."

Masuto had his notebook out. "Feuilletés à la crème? What are those?"

"Pastry horns with a cream or custard filling."

"And the strawberry tarts would also have some sort of custard base?"

"Yes."

"And what did you do with the rest of the pastry?"

"As I said, I threw it away—into the garbage. I adore such pastry. I put it beyond temptation."

"And the garbage? Is it still here?"

"It was picked up yesterday."

"What about the box in which the pastry came? Did Ana take the box with her?"

"No. We wrapped her three éclairs in aluminum foil."

"Then you have the box?" Masuto said eagerly.

"I'm afraid not. When I threw the pastry away, it was box and all. If I had only known. You don't think that whatever bakery it was is just spreading this food poisoning all over the place?"

"No, I doubt that. But about the box—tell me about it. Was there any printing on it, the name of the bakery perhaps?"

"No, it was just one of those plain cardboard boxes that bakeries put their pastry in."

"This feuilleté stuff—is it common? Could you find it in many bakeries?"

"I wouldn't think so. There are really only four good pastry shops in this whole area. I should think it would have to come from one of those four."

"Could you give me the names?"

At that moment, the door bell sounded.

"That may be Detective Beckman," Masuto told her. "I asked him to meet me here." He followed her to the front door. Beckman, oversized, slope-shoulders, stood there shaking his head.

"Nothing, Masao."

"Wait here a moment, Sy."

She was standing behind him, watching intently. Not a foolish woman by any means. The tendency to regard any wealthy divorced woman as an empty-headed fool was something Masuto did not share. "I want to write down the names of those four bakeries," he said to her. "Could I have a few minutes alone with Detective Beckman? Then if I can impose on you a little more?"

"Yes, of course."

She opened the door wider and asked Beckman to step in. Then she gave Masuto the names of the bakeries. "I'll be in the study," she said to him.

"Thank you."

They stood inside the door, Beckman looking around the place curiously. "Eight-and-a-half bucks for a pound of candy," he said reflectively.

"And you got nothing?"

"Would you believe, Masao, that they sold twenty-four boxes of the stuff already today, and it ain't two o'clock yet? What is it with money? Has it gone out of style?"

"You pushed them?"

"Sure I pushed them, but there is no way in the world they could give me anything worth a damn. We don't know when the candy was bought—maybe last week, maybe a month ago. It's a standard box, each one the same as the next."

"I figured that's the way it would be."

"Great. I got nothing else to do with my time."

"Now you have. Here are the names of four bakeries. That's just a beginning, but hit these four first. Two days ago, a pastry carton was delivered to this address—three chocolate éclairs, three strawberry tarts, and two things called feuilletés. I have it written down here. These feuilletés are pastry horns with a cream filling. That narrows it. I'll see you back at headquarters."

Masuto closed the door behind Beckman and went into the study. Laura Crombie stood in one corner of the room, and she stared at Masuto unhappily as he entered.

"There's more to this than just a case of food poisoning, isn't there?"

"I'm afraid so."

"Have you had lunch, Mr. Masuto?" she asked unexpectedly.

"It's not important."

"I think it is. I can give you scrambled eggs and coffee."

"Thank you, but I can't impose on you."

"You certainly can. I'm hungry too. And I'm frightened. Do you know how often a woman who lives alone in this strange society of ours is frightened? I'm frightened right now at the thought of what you are going to tell me. And you must tell me, I suppose?"

"I must—yes."

Masuto sat at the big wooden table in her kitchen, watching her prepare eggs and coffee and toast. She moved deftly. She was a competent woman.

"You have no family?"

"None. I'm alone in the world. I had a daughter."

"Oh?"

"She died." Shortly and thrust aside. She had no desire to talk about the daughter who had died. "Do you like your eggs soft or well done?"

"Either way. Tell me about these women who are your bridge friends."

"Don't you think you should first tell me what this is all about?" When Masuto hesitated, she added, "You probably pride yourself on being inscrutable. Well, Nisei or not, you've given me a feeling of disaster ever since you entered this house."

"You're very sensitive, Mrs. Crombie."

"Or frightened. I overheard you talking to the

other detective. I wasn't eavesdropping. His voice carries."

"I know."

"Alice called me this morning."

"Alice Greene?" It was Masuto's turn to be surprised. "Was she one of your bridge partners?"

"Yes. And her dog ate some candy and died. Lubie candy. You don't get food poisoning from candy. Not from Lubie's candy."

"No, you don't."

"Then I think it's time you let me in on what is happening to us."

"All right. Ana Fortez died of a type of food poisoning called botulism. Do you know what that is?"

"Only that it's very deadly."

"Very deadly. It begins with a bacillus that produces a poisonous toxin. Now there are various types of stomach disorders that can result from eating a bad éclair, but botulism is not one of them. Botulism can only be produced when the bacillus is in an airtight area, and it is almost always the result of putrified meat or badly canned vegetables, not éclairs."

She shook her head in bewilderment. "I don't understand you, Sergeant. You told me that Ana had died from eating the éclairs that I gave her."

"So she did. And she died of botulism. I would guess that the éclairs were intended for you or your guests. I would also guess that the rest of the pastry was equally deadly."

"But you said—"

"That you can't have a natural botulin in an éclair. That's right. I would still be guessing, but I would suppose that someone grew the botulism toxin and injected the pastry with it."

"Oh, my God! But why? Why?"

"We'll get to that. Right now, I would like you to telephone Mrs. Greene and the other two women you played bridge with and suggest to them that they refrain from eating anything sent to them or delivered to them, regardless of its origin—at least until I can arrange to speak to them."

There was a telephone on the kitchen wall. Laura Crombie started to say something, then swallowed her words, stared at Masuto, hesitated, and then went to the telephone. Masuto watched her and listened.

"Just do as I say. . . . Please. . . . No, I can't explain over the phone. . . . I'm sitting here with a policeman and he says he will see you and explain everything. . . . Yes, it has something to do with Ana's death. . . . Yes, I'm frightened too."

The other calls followed more or less the same pattern, and when Laura Crombie returned to the kitchen table, Masuto pushed his pad and pen toward her. "Please give me their names and addresses." Her hand was shaking as she attempted to write. "I'll write them," Masuto said gently. "Suppose we start with Alice Greene."

He put down name, address, and telephone number. Next, Nancy Legett, and then Mitzie Fuller.

"Tell me about them," Masuto said. "How you met them, how long you know them."

She didn't respond. As if she had only this moment realized it, she whispered, "Someone is trying to kill us. All of us. Isn't that what you're telling me?"

"No!" he said sharply. "That's not what I'm telling you. At this moment, I have no idea what is going on, whether this is some stupid joke, some monstrous prank, or whatever."

"No, no, no." She took a deep breath and got hold

of herself. "I am not going to be hysterical, Sergeant Masuto, but if you want me to be frank and open with you, then you must be quite frank with me. For all I know, you may be convinced that I am behind all this, that I poisoned Ana and that I sent the candy to Alice. After all, you have only my word about the pastry being delivered here."

"Did you poison Ana Fortez?" Masuto asked matter-of-factly.

"No! Of course not!" Masuto looked at her with a slight smile. "Don't you believe me?" she demanded.

"It's of no consequence whether I believe you or not. If it makes you feel better, I will say I believe you. That doesn't help us. I must find out who is doing this, whether it is you or someone else."

"That's very comforting."

"I think Ana's death was an accident. That lets you out, doesn't it? If you had known that the pastry was poisoned, you would not have given it to her."

"Yes, that makes sense—thank God. Why didn't you say that before?"

"I was making a point. I want you to help me, and you can help me better if you have no predetermined notions. Now tell me about your bridge partners."

"You know their names, Alice Greene, Nancy Legett, and Mitzie Fuller. Alice is a tall, beautiful blonde—"

"Please, forgive me," Masuto interrupted. "Let me ask direct questions. Then it will not take so long. I will see them," he explained, "so I will know what they look like."

"Yes, of course you will."

"First—age?"

"Yes. Alice is thirty-six. Nancy goes on being thirty-nine. She's forty-two. And Mitzie—well, I really don't know. I would guess twenty-seven or twenty-eight."

"Why the uncertainty about Mitzie? You're so sure of the others."

"The others are old friends. I hardly know Mitzie."

"Oh? Then how did she come into the bridge game?"

"I got to talking with her at the hairdresser. She was in the next chair, and she appeared to be a nice kid, and we needed a fourth—as a matter of fact she's a very good player, and she's played a lot of duplicate."

"What hairdresser?"

"Tony Cooper's on Camden."

Masuto jotted it down. "You said you were divorced. May I ask when?"

"Two years—well, only a year since I filed. Before that it was a separation. You didn't ask my age. I'm forty-five."

"I would have thought younger," Masuto said. "Your first marriage?"

"My second. My first husband died of a heart attack twelve years ago. I married Arthur Crombie three years ago."

"The real estate man?"

"Yes, do you know him?"

"I know about him—just the things one hears and reads. I have to be indelicate. How much alimony does he pay you?"

"None. Anything Arthur Crombie touches comes up gold. Six months after we were married, my father died. I was the only heir, and the estate was worth millions. I gave Arthur half of it. It was a stiff price to pay to get him out of my life, but well worth it."

"You're not fond of him?"

"He's a bastard, period. But if you're thinking that he'd want to kill me, well, no way. He has the money and he knows he's not in my will. He couldn't care less whether I'm alive or dead."

"Where is your will?"

"You mean, where do I keep it? Somewhere in the study. Does it matter?"

"Perhaps. Tell me about the others. Are they all married?"

"All divorced. Does that surprise you?" She had reacted to the expression on Masuto's face. "You see, we're all in the same boat—shock, boredom, frustration. Certainly four divorced women in Beverly Hills are not that unusual."

"Could you give me the names of the husbands—the ex-husbands?"

"Yes—"

He had his notebook ready.

"You think—one of them?" she asked slowly.

"I don't know what to think—yet."

"But why all of us? If we had eaten the pastry, it would have been all of us. Why? What sense does it make?"

"I don't know. Suppose we start with Mrs. Greene."

"She was married to Alan Greene. He operates a chain of clothing stores. The big one is down on Wilshire."

Masuto nodded.

"Nancy," Laura Crombie went on, "was married to Fulton Legett, the film producer. That's a rotten story. They were married in New York about twenty-two years ago. He was a gofer at ABC television. Nancy worked as a secretary at the same company. Then he quit to try TV production. For years she supported him and took his garbage. He's one of those angry, aggressive, ambitious little bastards. Then Nancy's mother died and left her sixty thousand dollars, and she gave it to Fulton and he used it as seed money to produce *Flames*—"

"Seed money?"

"Start-up money—to option the property and pay a writer to do a screenplay. The film was a hit, and suddenly Fulton was a millionaire. They moved out here and bought a house on Lexington Road. Then two more big hits, and Fulton was a millionaire and Nancy was forty and not very attractive anymore. At that point, you trade the forty for the two twenties. Fulton dumped her. The wages of virtue."

Masuto nodded and scribbled in his notebook.

"And then there's Mitzie. She's a beauty and a doll. You can't feel sorry for her. She was married to Bill Fuller, the director. It lasted six months. She doesn't talk about it or him, but from what I've heard he's a louse."

She was hardly reticent in her judgments, Masuto decided, and said thoughtfully, "You don't like men very much, do you?"

"Don't misjudge me. We're not talking about the genus. We're talking about four men. I don't like any of them."

"Do you know where Fuller is working now?"

"I think Mitzie mentioned he's doing a film at Metro."

"I see."

Masuto closed his notebook and stared at Laura Crombie thoughtfully. "Suppose I said that all four of you are in very great danger."

"I'd believe you."

"Would the others?"

"I could convince them."

"Could you be convincing enough to have them all here tonight?"

"If they haven't made other plans."

"Even if they have, I want them here. It's very important."

"At what time?"

"Say ten o'clock—and if I'm late, please wait for me. And until then, I'd like them to stay indoors and not to let any strangers into their houses. I'd like you to do the same. And again remind them about the food. Will you do that for me?"

"All right. But this is crazy—absolutely crazy."

"I know," Masuto said gently. "Much of the world is crazy, but this is where we are."

Chapter 3

OMI SAIKU

When Masuto walked into police headquarters on Rexford Drive, the city manager was there talking to Wainwright, and Wainwright nodded for Masuto to join them.

"What I want to know," Wainwright was saying, "is how the hell this stuff gets out. There are no blabbermouths here. Masuto and Beckman are on it, and they don't talk."

"Frank Lubie called me. He smelled something in Beckman's questions. He was sore as hell at even the implication that something would be wrong with his candy. You know, he has a point. If what you tell me gets out, it could ruin him. He's not only a sizable taxpayer, but his factory's here in town."

"Can we put a lid on it?" Wainwright asked Masuto. "What do you think?"

Masuto shrugged. "The vet knows. Mrs. Greene knows. They know down at L.A.P.D. It's not just a question of the candy. It's a lot more than that."

"What's a lot more?" the city manager asked.

"We have a poor Mexican kid murdered by some lunatic who seems determined to kill four other women. Ana Fortez was a mistake. If any of the others die, I don't think it will be a mistake."

"Four women!" Wainwright exclaimed. "What the devil are you talking about?"

Briefly, Masuto summed up his conversation with Laura Crombie.

"I know Mrs. Crombie," the city manager said. "You're making an inference, Masuto. It could all be some kind of accident. What's the point in scaring these women to death?"

"They won't die of fright. Other things are more deadly," Masuto replied.

"I think you're out of line—way out of line."

"Hold on," Wainwright said. "I'll agree that Masao is guessing. But I've had experience with his guesses. Usually they come off pretty good."

"You mean you agree with this notion that some lunatic is trying to kill these four women? Why? Because they play bridge together? For Christ's sake, Wainwright, this is Beverly Hills!"

"That doesn't give us any exemption from crazies," Wainwright said.

"All right. If you buy it, what do you intend to do about it?" the city manager asked.

"I don't know. We could put cops at their houses. What do you think, Masao?"

Masuto shrugged. "For how long? A week, a month? You get something like this with no reason and no motive and no direction—well, I don't know. I think those women are in danger, terrible danger. But I don't know why or how."

"If we don't and something happens," the city manager said, "I get the backlash."

"And if they go out of their homes, if they go shopping or on a date, does the cop follow them?" Masuto asked. "We don't know what we're dealing with, and until we know something more, it's not going to help to put cops outside their houses. Anyone who is crazy-smart enough to get hold of botulism toxin is smart enough to get around a cop standing outside a house."

"All right, get on it," the captain said to Masuto. "You'll be talking to those women?"

"Tonight."

Beckman was waiting in Masuto's office. His broad, heavy face had what Masuto thought of as his "mission accomplished" look.

"You found the bakery?" Masuto asked.

"Right. La Consoler on Third Street," Beckman answered.

Masuto couldn't help smiling.

"The owners of the bakery don't think it's funny. They're sore as hell. They're going to sue the city," Beckman said.

"I was smiling at the name. It means to console, to comfort."

"Well, that's what they do. You could eat yourself into an early grave at the place. They're the only outfit in this part of the city that makes those fuel—what do you call them?"

"Feuilletés."

"Right. First they couldn't be bothered, and then I had to lean a little and tell them about the Fortez kid."

"I wish you hadn't."

"Masao, there was no other way. They just brushed it off until I got serious. There were maybe twenty customers in the place. My God, don't they eat nothing but cake in this town? Then the manager took me behind the store, and we called the clerks in one by one. One of them was an old lady of about seventy, and, believe it or not, she remembered. Do you know why?"

"Why?"

"Because it was a Mexican kid and he just handed her a slip of paper which specified the pastry. It came to seven dollars and seventy-five cents for eight pieces of pastry, would you believe it? He gave her a ten-dollar bill."

"A Chicano kid. Just that. What did he look like?"

"Maybe fourteen, fifteen years old. What does a Chicano kid of that age look like? Blue jeans, tee shirt, dark skin, dark eyes, black hair—"

"There are at least a thousand like that within five miles of here," Masuto said with annoyance.

"Can I help that, Masao? At least the old lady remembered."

"I'm sore at myself, not at you."

"They'll be calling the city manager," Beckman said.

"He'll have a busy day. Did the saleswoman keep the slip of paper on which the order was written?"

"I thought of that. No. The kid asked to have it back. It's open and shut, Masao. X drives up in his car, sees the kid, gives him the paper and a ten-dollar bill. Buy the cake and keep the change."

"It could be. And that might just mean that the kid hangs out in the neighborhood. So get over there, Sy, and ask around. One Chicano kid knows another. Take a couple of bills from expenses, and buy a little information. It's the only thread we have, a damn thin one."

"I'll try," Beckman agreed. "Where will you be?"

"Downtown with Omi. I'm curious about botulism."

Beverly Hills, like many other small cities in Los

Angeles County, has limited police resources. The country tends to regard Los Angeles County as a single metropolitan area, but in reality it encloses more than seventy towns and cities, as well as a considerable unincorporated area. Most of the small cities in the county have their own police forces; some depend on the sheriff's office, which polices the unincorporated areas of the county; and then to one degree or another, many of the small towns depend for additional resources on the police force of the city of Los Angeles, the largest metropolitan area in the county. Omi Saiku ran the poison laboratory for the Los Angeles Police Department. He was a small, cheerful man whose dark eyes peered out of heavy glasses. He welcomed Masuto into his tiny room, a single table, a single chair, and shelves of mysterious bottles.

As Masuto entered, Omi rose from the microscope into which he had been peering and said, "Ah, estimable cousin, you deign at last to visit my house of horrors."

"Wainwright calls that kind of talk my Charlie Chan routine," Masuto replied sourly.

"Ah so. He does not distinguish between the Chinese and the Japanese. A Western failing. Did you know that Roshi Azuki is in Los Angeles? Tomorrow he will attend za-zen at the Zen Center. Can you join us?"

"Tomorrow I'll be looking for a homicidal maniac."

"Yes. Of course. Your botulism man."

"Man?" Masuto demanded. "Why man? Why not woman?"

"Because no woman would kill in such a manner."

"Why not?"

"I have been in this room for twelve years," Omi said. "The poison homicides and suicides of the whole state reach me eventually. There are patterns. Strychnine is the most common and the most frequently used by women. Now what is a poison, Masao? Strictly but generally speaking, it is any substance that causes change in the molecular structure of an organ. That's not difficult. It's less a question of substance than of quantity. Alcohol, morphine, cocaine, nicotine are all deadly in sufficient quantity. But according to my records, ninety-five percent of women murderers do not plot bizarre poisonings. Driven to desperation, they take whatever is at hand, arsenic, found in Paris green, phosphorus in rat poison, and of course strychnine, easily come by. The fancy poisoning is done by men, and by golly this botulism of yours is the fanciest I've seen in a long while. Now take this bacillus botulinus. Why do we see so little of it? Why are whole populations not ravaged by its poisonous toxin? Thank mother nature, who always gives with one hand and takes away with the other. In other words, bacillus botulinus is anaerobic."

"Which means what?"

"Simply that it will not grow in the presence of air. It requires low temperature and airlessness. Now don't think that you can take a piece of meat, let it putrefy, exclude the air, and grow a botulin. Maybe yes, maybe no—most likely no. To grow a botulin, you require the botulism bacillus, and since it cannot live in the presence of air, the likelihood is that you won't get it. The only place it seems to turn up these days is in canned goods, and even there it's only one out of a thousand bad cans that produces a botulinus. But here, honored cousin, here we have something unique—not the putrefaction which produces the botulinus, which in turn produces the deadly toxin, no indeed—here we have the toxin itself, no putrefaction, no source, simply the deadly poison. And that, my dear Masao, is the work of a chemist. Find the chemist and you find your murderer."

"Thank you," Masuto said without delight.

"Or conceivably a pharmacologist."

"I am most grateful."

Masuto bade his cousin good-bye and descended to the floor below, moving through the vast machinery of the Los Angeles Police Department, wondering how it might be to work for an organization like this rather than for the police force of a small town of thirty thousand population. He found Lieutenant Pete Bones at his desk, painfully pecking out a report on his typewriter. Bones, a heavy-set, thick-necked man in his forties, turned his pale blue, suspicion-clouded eyes on Masuto and then grinned.

"Ah, my favorite Oriental sleuth. How goes it in the pastures of the rich?"

"Too much time on their hands. The result is murder most foul."

"That's a quote from somewhere. I retire in two years. The wife and I have a cabin, if you can call it that, up at Mammoth. I'm going to read all the books I never read being a cop. You'll come and visit us, Masao."

"With pleasure."

"And what can I do for you now?"

"Can you set the machinery to work? I'm looking for a chemist or a pharmacologist with a criminal record, probably in this area, but maybe upstate."

"Masao, you can make a San Francisco request as easy as we can. I can put it into work here. I'll tell you this. We got to come up with at least ten names, maybe more."

"I can narrow it," Masuto said. "The one I'm looking for—well, I think he'll be killed, either today or tomorrow or the next day."

"What!"

"Possibly yesterday, but more likely today or tomorrow."

"Wait a minute, wait a minute! You're asking me to look for a chemist with a criminal record who's going to be murdered? Come on, Masao, come on! Who's going to kill him?"

"I don't know."

"You don't know who this chemist is, or maybe he's a pharmacist, but you don't know who he is or where he is or which he is, but you know he's going to be killed, but you don't know who's going to kill him. Do you know how crazy that sounds?"

"Pretty crazy, yes."

"Then how in hell do you know he's going to be killed?"

"I don't know. I said I think so. I'm dealing with a killer, and I try to put myself into his mind and think the way he thinks. It's not easy. You get a crime of passion or violence, and you can understand it. They are crimes done by human beings who have momentarily lapsed. But this is something coldly plotted by a man who has stopped being human. So I try to approximate that kind of mind. I have to. It's all we have, not one damn thing more. If I can find this chemist while he's alive, it will help, maybe wind the thing up. Even dead, it will help."

"Okay," Bones agreed. "I'll set things moving in the county. You can line up the San Francisco cops from Beverly Hills."

"I don't think it's up there. I think it's right here in L.A."

At that moment, a uniformed policeman approached them, looked at Masuto curiously, and then asked, "Are you Sergeant Masuto, Beverly Hills P.D.?"

Masuto nodded.

"We got a call for you."

Bones picked up his telephone and told them to put through Sergeant Masuto's call. He handed the phone to Masuto, and Beckman's voice said, "Masao, is that you?"

"What's up, Sy?"

"Can you get away now?"

"If it's important."

"It's important. I'm up on Mulholland Drive, half a mile west of Laurel Canyon. You'll see my car and a sheriff's car and an L.A.P.D. car. I'm trying to get them not to touch anything or move anything until you get here, and they're giving me a hard time because it's their turf, not ours. But I think I can hold them if you get here in half an hour."

"What have you got?"

"I got a body. But get up here and we'll talk about it."

Chapter 4

THE CHICANO KID

Mulholland Drive is a narrow, twisting, badly-paved two-lane road that runs across the ridge of the Santa Monica Mountains and the Hollywood Hills, from Cahuenga Canyon in the east to Topanga Canyon in the west. Although it is almost entirely contained within the city limits of Los Angeles, it presents a vista of wild brush and mesquite-covered hills as well as breathtaking views of both the city of Los Angeles and the San Fernando Valley—providing one drives it on a day when the smog is light enough to see anything at all. Nevertheless, its illusion of wilderness, combined with the fact that it bisects one of the most heavily populated cities in the United States, makes it a favorite scenic drive for tourists and a weekend outing place for the local residents.

At least twice a year, preferably during the winter months when there was little or no smog, Masuto's wife Kati would pack a picnic lunch, and he would drive her and the two children to one of the lookout points on Mulholland. There they would eat their lunch and marvel at the great vista of valley and mountains spread out before them. He thought of this now as he raced along the Hollywood Freeway, his siren screaming—a sound he disliked intensely—his old Datsun shivering in protest against eighty miles an hour. He had to cut his speed as he turned off for Mulholland. Not quite half an hour, but forty-one minutes from the time he had received Beckman's phone call in downtown Los Angeles to the cluster of cars on Mulholland was not bad time at all.

From a group of uniformed officers—there was a sheriff's deputy and three L.A.P.D. cops, while a fourth uniformed officer waved the traffic on—Masuto heard Beckman's booming voice: "There's Masuto now. So you let the body lay there for an extra half hour. The kid's dead. He's not going to be any more dead."

A white-coated ambulance man said, "You kept us sitting here like this was the only stiff in Los Angeles."

"You got a radio. Stop yapping," Beckman said.

"Are you Sergeant Masuto?" one of the Los Angeles cops asked him.

"Yes."

"Well, this ain't Beverly Hills. You can't interfere like this. I damn near arrested that guy Beckman," the cop said.

"It connects with our trouble. He wouldn't let you move the body, is that it?" Masuto asked.

"That's it. So will you go down there and see whatever he wants you to see and let us get out of here?"

"Down here, Masao," Beckman said.

Beckman clambered down the mesquite-covered hillside, Masuto picking his way after him. Another ambulance man, holding a stretcher, stood in a tiny hollow where the body was wedged. It was a young Chicano boy, dressed in tee shirt, jeans, and sneakers.

"Shot once in the head, behind the ear—small caliber, maybe a twenty-two," Beckman said.

"How long has he been dead?" Masuto asked the ambulance man. "Can you make a guess?"

"At least two days."

"Some kids climbed down here and they spotted the body," Beckman told him. "It doesn't have to be our kid. This city's filled with kids who do violence on each other, and maybe ten thousand of them wear blue jeans and tee shirts. But look up there at the broken branches, Masao."

Masuto nodded. "Dumped over the side, out of a car."

"That's right. He gets into the car after he buys the pastry. Maybe he delivers it."

"No. It had to be injected with the botulin. He didn't deliver the pastry." Masuto stared at the body again. "Chicano kids are killed, but not this way. Gang wars, bursts of violence. But not this way."

"Can we get him out of here now?" the ambulance man asked.

Masuto nodded, and he and Beckman climbed back up to the road.

"Well, thank God that's over," the L.A. cop in charge said.

"What did he have in his pockets?" Masuto asked.

"We got to hold it for the investigators," the cop replied.

"I know. Can we look at it?"

"Not much to look at. Just some money. Nothing else. No identification."

"How much money?"

"Here," he said, handing Masuto an envelope. "Count it yourself."

Masuto counted it. "Twelve dollars and twenty-five cents," he told Beckman. "It fits. He gave the kid another ten dollars. I suppose he invented another errand, and that's how he got the kid into the car."

"It could be. He's one cold-blooded bastard, Masao."

"Do you buys know something about this killing?" the L.A. cop asked. "If you do, one of you ought to hang around until the investigators show up."

"When will that be?"

"Any time now. We run a busy city. It's not Beverly Hills."

"We getting there," Beckman said. "Don't put down Beverly Hills."

"You stay with it," Masuto said to Beckman. "Tail after the investigators. You can tell them what we've got, which is nothing. I don't remember one like this. We have nothing—no lead, no motive, no direction."

"We know one thing," Beckman said.

"What's that?"

"That this son of a bitch kills people the way we kill flies."

"He's insane. So are a thousand others walking around on the streets of this city. It doesn't help now. Maybe later. See what you can find out about the kid. It's possible that our killer just picked him up on the street; it's also possible that they had a previous acquaintance. Maybe the kid had friends and one of them saw something. It's just barely possible that the money is a coincidence—possible, but not likely. So if you have a chance, poke around the bakery again. Get a death picture. I hate to use them, but someone around the bakery might recognize it."

"I can get the bakery lady down to the L.A. morgue."

"I wouldn't put an old lady through that. Get the picture and show it to her. That ought to do it."

"Where will you be?"

"Damned if I know," Masuto said, shaking his

head. "I'll be at Laura Crombie's house, but not until ten o'clock tonight." Then he added, "I'll call in. You'd better do the same."

Masuto went back to his car, sat for a moment or two staring through the windshield, then took out his notebook and called headquarters on his radiophone.

"Polly," he said to the lady who answered the phone, "this is Masao. Jot down this number." He gave it to her. "Dial it and patch it through to me."

"For you, Masao, it's a pleasure."

He always reacted in surprise at the fact that women liked him. He never thought of himself as likeable or lovable, a tall, dour-faced second generation Japanese man, yet nothing pleased him more than this almost consistent response on the part of women. He pardoned himself; he argued to himself that he had a good wife whom he loved, that he was scrupulous in his behavior as a policeman, that he was content. Or was he?

This was no time to debate it. Laura Crombie's voice came over the phone.

"This is Sergeant Masuto, Mrs. Crombie. There was a question I didn't ask—at least I can't remember asking it. Who received the pastry when it was delivered?"

"Didn't I tell you? Ana did."

"And of course she never mentioned who delivered it?"

"No. It wouldn't be of any importance."

"Yes. And since I left you, anything?"

"No, nothing out of the ordinary. I called the ladies. They'll all be here."

"I'd like to change that," Masuto said.

"Oh, no!"

"Please. I'd like you to call them again and get

them to your house right now. And then I'm going to have a policeman sitting in his car across the street from your house."

"But why?"

"I'll tell you why very bluntly and plainly—becuase I'm afraid."

"Sergeant Masuto, we don't live in a jungle. This is Beverly Hills."

"I know it is. Will you please do as I say?"

"I suppose so. When will you be here?"

"About ten, as I said."

"And we just sit here and wait for you? Come on, you can't be serious!"

"I am very serious. I know what I ask is a nuisance, but I'm trying to keep you alive—all of you."

"Aren't you being dramatic?"

"I hope so. Enough to impress you."

He finished with Laura Crombie and was talking to Polly again when Beckman came over to the car and stood by the open window. Masuto had just asked her to get a make from L.A.P.D. on Tony Cooper.

"Who's Tony Cooper?" Beckman asked him.

"A hairdresser. You've seen his place on Camden Road."

"How does he fit into all this?"

"I don't know. I look where the light is, because everywhere else it's dark."

"And what's that supposed to mean?"

"Not every much. They tell the story of a man crawling around under a lamp post on his hands and knees. Another man stops and asks him why, and the man on his hands and knees says that he lost a gold cufflink. "Where did you lose it?" the man asks, and the man on his hands and knees replies that he lost it a hundred fect down the street. 'Then why are you looking here?' the second man asks. And the man who lost the cufflink replies, 'Because it's light here.' "

"That don't make much sense," Beckman said.

"What does in this crazy case? There are your investigators," Masuto said, pointing to where a car had pulled up. "Give it about an hour, Sy, and then I want you to drive over to Laura Crombie's place. I asked her to get the other three women over there, and they should be there by then. I don't want anyone else going into that house without your say-so."

"Come on, Masao, you can't do that. Wainwright would have my scalp if I tried anything like that."

"I'm not telling you to pull any rough stuff. We're putting the house under police protection. There's nothing illegal about that."

"What do you mean, we're putting it under police protection?"

"I'll fix it with Wainwright."

"So I see someone going in. Do I stop them?"

"No. Just find out why. Park near the door. If Mrs. Crombie says it's okay, let them in. But stay right on top of it, and don't take your eyes off that door for two minutes."

"That's great. When do you get there?"

"About ten. Maybe earlier—not later."

"And when do I eat?"

"Get a sandwich on the way. And grab those investigators. They've given it their five minutes."

"Masao," Beckman said, "why is L.A.P.D. the only police force in the country that calls its detectives investigators?"

"Ask them," Masuto said, and put his car in gear and drove off.

At Rexford Drive, Captain Wainwright listened bleakly to Masuto's account of the day's events.

"Assumptions," he said without enthusiasm. "All you got is a series of assumptions. We still don't know but maybe this Mexican girl died of the damn éclairs, and you link up the kid on Mulholland Drive with a group of wild guesses. You tell me we got a lunatic who's killed two people already, but all I see that I can put a finger on is a food poisoning and a killing that belongs to L.A.P.D."

"I beg to disagree. We have a murderer who is indifferent to human life. He's killed two people and a dog, and he'll kill anyone who stands in his way."

"What in hell do you mean, stands in his way? What is his way? What is he after?"

"I think he's after those four women. I think he's going to try to kill all four of them."

"Why?"

"I don't know. If I knew, we wouldn't be arguing. All I'm asking is that you give Beckman and me a free hand on this case."

"For how long?"

"As long as it takes—maybe another day, maybe a week. I don't know."

Wainwright sighed and nodded. "Okay, but don't talk to the press. Not a word. You want to make a murder case out of this, you can have the time. But keep it quiet." He stared intently at Masuto. "You keeping anything back?"

"Would I?"

"You damn well would. All right, it's yours."

Polly intercepted Masuto on his way out. She was small and blonde and blue-eyed. "What do I have to do," she asked him, "to get a reaction from Detective Sergeant Masuto?"

"You get it all the time. I hide it behind Oriental inscrutability."

"Which means?"

"That I adore you but don't dare show it."

"Bull. You are married. Every decent man is married. Try a singles bar some night and you'll see what I mean. Don't you want to know what downtown has to say about your Tony Cooper?"

"That's what I asked."

"Well, here it is." She read from a slip of paper. "Three arrests, homosexual practice, no convictions, all of it ten years ago. You know, it should be the women who do the resenting, not the cops. We suffer when the men leave the market place, and as far as I'm concerned the cops have got better things to do than to pull people in for being gay. You know how they do it?"

"I have heard," Masuto said.

"They entice them into porno movie houses and then arrest them. I think it stinks. Our boys wouldn't do that, would they, Masao?"

"No, we're too short on cops. Thanks, Polly."

It was almost six o'clock when Masuto parked on Camden Drive across the street from the beauty parlor, but the shop was still open. Only a single customer remained, a brown head being trimmed by a slender, dark man in a white jacket with pink stripes. Masuto crossed the street and entered the shop.

"We don't do men and we're closed," the man in the striped blazer told him.

"Tony Cooper?" Masuto stood just inside the door.

"That's right." He stared at Masuto thoughtfully, and then said to the woman in the chair, "Don't move, baby. I'll be with you in a minute." Then he walked over to Masuto and whispered, "Fuzz?"

Masuto nodded.

"Oriental fuzz. I'll be damned." Still in a whisper, "Can you come back? She's the end of the line."

"I'll wait."

Masuto sat down and picked up a copy of *Architectural Digest* and leafed through the pages. You could gauge the prices at a hairdressing establishment by the kind of magazines they left around. *Architectural Digest* probably indicated a twenty-five- or thirty-dollar haircut. It was part of the trivia that went into Masuto's store of facts. A policeman living very simply in a small house in Culver City—which is to Beverly Hills what Brooklyn is to Fifth Avenue—he did his daily work in one of the wealthiest communities on the face of the earth. It called for a certain kind of balance and a special kind of perspective, and he thought of this as he leafed through the magazine, looking at photographs of the homes of millionaires. He had never envied wealth, although often enough he pitied those who possessed it; but then, he was a Zen Buddhist, and that gave him his own unique handle on things. Sy Beckman handled it by ignoring it; it just happened to be the shop where he worked.

Cooper finished with the lady whose hair he had been cutting and saw her to the door. Then he turned to Masuto and shook his head. "You guys never give up, do you?"

"I try not to, but if you're thinking about your record, I couldn't care less." He showed his badge. "Masuto, Beverly Hills police."

"Okay, but what can I do for you? Is it a violation or tickets to the annual ball?"

"Neither. I want to pick your brains, and I want whatever I pick to stay with you, because if any of it gets out, I will come back and lean on you very heavily."

"Now?" he demanded indignantly. "It's a quarter after six. I'm closing. I've had a hard, lousy day. The help goes home at five, but if some broad wants a haircut at six, I stay."

"Now."

"I got a date."

"Call them and tell them you'll be late."

"I don't have to answer any questions."

"I don't have to be nice," Masuto said gently.

"All right. You win. You want coffee?"

"Yes, thank you."

Cooper regarded him curiously. "You're a damn funny cop. I never knew they had a Jap on the police force here."

"You live and you learn."

"I shouldn't have said that—Jap," Cooper said. "I meant Japanese. What the hell, you pick it up. I'll get the coffee. Maybe you want a drink?"

Masuto shook his head, and Cooper went to the back of the place and then emerged with two cups.

"Sugar and cream?"

"Just straight."

He handed Masuto the coffee and sat down beside him. "Since that lousy film came out, everyone thinks this business has class and glamour. It doesn't. You work your ass off and take crud all day. I been on my feet nine hours."

"A man should enjoy his work," Masuto said.

"Do you enjoy yours?"

"At times, yes. Right now, no."

"Where do I fit in?"

"Here are four names: Laura Crombie, Alice Greene, Nancy Legett, and Mitzie Fuller. How many of these women do you know?"

"I know all of them."

"Oh? And how is that?"

"They're customers."

"I'd like to know about them."

"I don't talk about my customers. I got maybe two or three principles. That's one of them."

Masuto smiled. "That's admirable. But I'm a cop, and these four women are in great danger. So in this instance, I suggest you put your principles aside."

"What kind of danger?"

"Someone is trying to kill them. I'll telling you this because I think it's the only way I'll get you to open up, but it stops with you."

The hairdresser stared at Masuto. "Are you putting me on?"

"No. I'm telling you the truth."

"Who? Who's trying to kill them?"

"I don't know. It could even be you."

Cooper shook his head slowly. "Not likely. Oh, I hate some of these biddies enough to want to kill them, but it's not my style. I couldn't kill a mouse. Anyway, I'm a vegetarian."

Masuto did not regard it as a non sequitur. "You're not a likely suspect, but you do know all four of them."

"Customers. I know maybe two or three hundred dames in this town. Mostly they don't bother me. I take them for what they are. They take me for what I am. It doesn't drive them out of their minds to have their hair cut by a guy who's gay. It's only the cops and Anita Bryant who climb walls at the thought that somebody maybe don't have the same sexual preference."

"How well do you know them?"

"The way a hairdresser knows his customers. Some more, some less."

"Start with Laura Crombie."

"She doesn't talk much. I don't know whether I like her or not but she's straight on. She doesn't dye her hair."

"Who would want to kill her?"

"You're asking me? She doesn't even take alimony from the son of a bitch she was married to."

"How do you know that?"

"The women talk."

"Do you know her husband?"

"Just by reputation. Crombie and Hawkes, real estate."

"Who is Hawkes?"

"Nobody. He's been dead for years."

"Alice Greene?"

"Tall willowy blonde. Not real, but a great head of hair. She's the type I'd go for if I were straight. Real class, except that a buck is a buck. No other reason why she married that creep Alan Greene—you can't turn on the tube without seeing his ads for his string of stores. Since I'm talking, I'll talk. Her alimony is five grand a month. I know some guys who'd murder their own mothers to save sixty thousand a year, and to add insult to injury she's been having an affair with Monte Sweet, the comic. But they'll never get married. They'd have to be crazy to kill the goose that laid the golden egg."

"Meaning her alimony."

"You bet your ass. The best investment there is. You put in a couple of years, and not only have you got the community property law going for you, but you got a fat check coming in every month."

"And is that the case with Nancy Legett?"

"Now there's something else. She's a quiet little mouse—the one in ten in Beverly Hills who just lets her hair go gray. I don't know what to make of her—quiet, polite, no gossip. She was married twenty-two years to Fulton Legett, the producer. He's a big swinger, and for a long time he was up on top. But the past few years, he's had one bomb on top of another, and today they say he's broke. That don't mean he's poor, but maybe he's tired of keeping her in that big house up on Lexington Road. She's got three kids. They're away at school, the way I hear it, two of them in swanky Eastern colleges and one in a prep school back east. That don't come cheap."

"And Mitzie Fuller?"

Tony Cooper leaned back and grinned. "Mitzie. She's a doll—she's an absolute doll. Red hair—real, not from the bottle—a great face and the best pair of boobs this side of the Grand Canyon. Never heard a bad word out of her. She is the sweetest, nicest bundle that ever walked into this tonsorial cathouse. Tell you something, Sarge, if I was straight I'd break my ass trying to get next to her. One thing about broads you can bet your last dollar on, the nicer they are, the worse bums they tie up with, and Mitzie's ex, Bill Fuller, is no exception to the rule."

"William Fuller, the director?"

"That's right. Now let me tell you something. I don't run the biggest hair shop in Beverly Hills, but I like to think it's the best, and I get the pick of the classy broads, and they talk and they talk and they talk. If I didn't have trouble writing my own name, I could write you a tome on the habits of so-called straight men that would curl your hair, and I'd have a chapter on film directors. They are the meanest, most arrogant, egotistical set of bastards that ever lived, and Billy Fuller is one of the top runners. I'm still waiting to hear something nice about him. Now I don't know why they got divorced, because Mitzie don't talk. They were only married six months when it broke up, but Mitzie got the house on Palm Drive, which the real estate ladies tell me is worth three-quarters of a million on today's market, and the word is that she gets a fat check every month. Well, she earned it. Six months living with Billy Fuller has no price on it. But you want a candidate, you got him. He's a killer. He'd kill anything that got in his way."

Masuto was silent for a long moment. Then he said, "I wouldn't mention that to anyone else—for your sake, as well as mine."

"You asked me."

"I know. And you told me. And for the time being, it rests with us. Right?"

"Right."

Chapter 5

THE L. A. COPS

Masuto stopped off for a hamburger and a cup of coffee, and he had them wrap two and fill a container of coffee for Beckman. Knowing Beckman, he knew that it would make no appreciable difference to Beckman's appetite if he had brought a sandwich to the vigil. For Beckman to sit in the car, preserving a sandwich for some future dinner hour, was unthinkable. He turned out to have been right.

"I'm starved," was the first thing Beckman said to him.

"I brought you two hamburgers and coffee."

"With pickles?"

"With pickles."

"You know," Beckman said as he unwrapped the first hamburger, "under that cold, inscrutable shell of yours, you got heart."

"I'm relieved to know that. What happened?"

"You mean with the kid or here?"

"First the kid."

"Well, we rounded up a couple of kids near the bakery, and they identified him. Jesus Consolo, fourteen years old. A good kid. Never got into any trouble, no dope, tenth grade, good marks. The L.A. investigators matched it up with a missing report, and I let them break the news to his parents. I'm no good for that kind of thing. I got a fourteen-year-old kid of my own, Masao, and I swear if I ever find that lunatic bastard—"

"No, you won't. Now what about the kids who identified him? Did they see anything?"

"Nothing, nothing—nothing until it stinks. This bastard leaves no loose ends."

"They all leave loose ends."

"I sure as hell hope so."

"And what about here?"

"Well, when I got here, I rang the bell and told Mrs. Crombie that I'd be here in the car. She wasn't crazy about the idea, and I asked her about the three other women, just to make sure they were inside."

"Were they?"

"Yeah, they're there. I told her to bolt the back door and to call me in case anyone came to the back door. That's it. All quiet as a graveyard."

"Good. Patch in a call to your wife and tell her you won't be home tonight."

"What? She'll skin me."

"I want you to stay overnight in the Crombie house."

"You're putting me on."

"Dead serious. I'm going to convince all four women to remain there overnight and I want you to stay with them."

"And that's what I tell my wife—that I'm sleeping in Beverly Hills with four dames?"

"If you want to be perfectly honest."

"Masao," Beckman said seriously, "I think you're a little nutty with this one. They don't need me there overnight. They lock the doors and the windows. Every one of these Beverly Hills houses has a burglar alarm system."

"I need you there."

"You're a heartless bastard."

"Am I? Locking you up with four lovely women—that's what every red-blooded American boy dreams of, or so I'm told."

"Okay, okay. When will you be back?"

"Before ten. Just hang in."

"I still don't know exactly what I'm supposed to do if someone comes to the door."

"Just find out who he is and what he wants. You don't keep him or her out. Let Mrs. Crombie decide about that."

Masuto's radio phone was speaking to him as he drove off. Wainwright's voice was demanding. "Where the hell are you, Masao?"

"Turning a corner two blocks away."

"Well, get over here. Do you know what time it is? It's eight o'clock, and I'm sitting here on my butt when I should be home eating a decent dinner, and I'm sitting here because the Los Angeles cops are sore as hell. They want your scalp and they want me here when they take it."

"I'll be there in two minutes."

"What in hell have you been up to?"

"Two minutes."

Masuto pulled into his parking space on Rexford Drive and went inside. Wainwright was pacing in front of Masuto's office. "What's this all about?" he snapped.

"I don't know. I have to call my wife."

"So help me, Masao, if there's one thing a crummy little police force like ours can't afford, it's a ruckus with the L.A. cops. Not now. Not with the city refusing to shell out a nickel for new equipment. We depend on those miserable bastards. I don't want them to mark us lousy."

"Who did you talk to?"

"A lieutenant, Pete Bones. He's coming up here with a Captain Kennedy."

"Pete's an old friend."

"He didn't sound like a friend, old or new."

"Let's take it easy and wait until they get here. Meanwhile, I have to call Kati, or I'll have more trouble than the Los Angeles cops could ever give me."

Masuto went into his office and dialed his home number. The first thing Kati said was, "Your dinner has spoiled."

"I'm sorry."

"I don't think you are. I think it's something you're saying. There are other policemen in the world and they work from nine to five and they see their children and their wives."

"You haven't gone to that women's consciousness-raising session yet?"

"I'm going tonight. I thought you would be here. Then when I realized you would not be here, I telephoned Suzi Asata, and she will be my baby sitter. I will have to pay her five dollars. I don't think it ought to come out of my household money. I think it ought to come out of your pocket."

"I agree with you," he said meekly.

"You do?"

"Yes. Why should that surprise you?"

"Oh, Masao, why do you make me so angry?"

"I don't think you're really angry."

"Please tell me that you will not do anything dangerous tonight."

"I promise you."

"And what will you do?"

"Only talk to some ladies."

"Stop teasing me. Why must you always tease me?"

"I'm not teasing. I promise to tell you the whole story when I see you. I am not talking to these ladies for pleasure. I am talking to them because they are part of this case I am on."

"I sometimes think that it is always a pleasure for you to talk to American ladies."

"Kati, I love you."

"Well—"

"Believe me. And how are the children?"

"Someday you will see them and decide for yourself."

He put down the phone as Polly entered. She was still small, blonde, and pretty. "I stayed an extra hour waiting for you, Masao."

"Oh?"

"I'm not making a pass. I'm saving that until you get divorced."

"I have no intention of getting divorced," he said severely.

"Baloney. All cops get divorced. Their wives can't put up with them. Anyway, we can save that discussion for another time. What I got for you now is a very funny phone call."

"Tell me about it."

"First place, foreign accent but phony."

"How do you know it was phony?"

She shrugged. "You watch enough TV, you know. He says to me, Who's on the poisoned candy case? Me, nobody tells me anything. I just answer the phone, and everything else I do, which is practically everything around here, it's guesswork. So I ask for his name, and he says Horst Brandt, to go with the phony German accent."

"Address?"

"Just as phony, I'm sure." She took a slip of paper from her purse and read him the address. It had a familiar ring, and Masuto consulted his notebook. It was Alice Greene's address on Roxbury Drive.

"Does it mean something?" Polly asked him.

"Maybe. Maybe not. You're sure he said candy? Nothing about éclairs?"

"What éclairs? Candy, éclairs. Nobody tells me a thing around here."

"And you're sure it was a man's voice, not a woman's?"

She stared at him in disgust. "What am I, Masao, a jerk, a nut? A man's voice. I told you that."

"I'm sorry. Go on."

"So I tell him that if it's a homicide case, it's Sergeant Masuto's department. Then he says, 'Masuto? You mean that Jap plainclothes cop?' He sort of forgets his accent too, and believe me, I get plenty steamed with that kind of talk and I'm ready to tell him to buzz off and sell his apples somewhere else, but I got enough sense to know that it may be important, so I tell him, yes, but we don't talk about people that way, and then he wants to talk to you, and I tell him you're not in but expected."

"Very interesting," Masuto said.

"Okay, I'm going. But if you don't tell me what this is all about tomorrow, I won't talk to you again."

"Promise. And thank you, Polly. Thank you for waiting."

"You can say that again."

For a few minutes after she had left, Masuto sat at his desk and stared at the door facing him. He was

still staring at it when Wainwright opened the door
and said shortly, "They're here. In my office."

Masuto followed Wainwright into the captain's office. Bones and Kennedy were seated. They made no
move to rise, nor did they smile or do any more than
nod their heads coldly. Kennedy was the very image
of a proper Los Angeles cop, about forty-five, trim,
handsome, sandy hair, cold blue eyes.

Bones opened the conversation by saying, "God
damn you, Masuto, we dragged our asses up here for
your cute tricks. Like we got nothing else to do with
our time."

Watching Masuto, Wainwright saw his dark eyes
harden, his mouth tighten. He had fought for Masuto
before, and he often said that Masuto was the best
cop he had on his force, but he also knew that
Masuto was unpredictable. Whereby he stepped into
the moment of silence and said, "Now, hold on,
Bones. I don't know what you and Kennedy are so
pissed off at, but you're in our town, and that calls
for a little bit of restraint. So suppose you tell us what
this is all about and we'll save the name-calling."

"I'll tell you what it's all about," Kennedy said
coldly. "Today this joker—" nodding at Masuto—
"comes downtown to get the advice of our poison lab,
which we don't begrudge him, and then he goes to
Peter here and tells Pete that a chemist whom he
doesn't identify but who has a criminal record is going
to be murdered. Then he walks out, and then two
hours later the man is murdered. Now what in hell
goes on? You don't want us to be pissed off? He's your
cop. Why the hell aren't you pissed off?"

Masuto watched Wainwright, who was trying to
repress a smile. "How does it stand?" Wainwright
asked. "Do you think Masuto killed him?"

"It could be."

"All right," Wainwright said tiredly. "You drove all the way up here from downtown and I missed my dinner and my wife is sore as hell. As far as Sergeant Masuto is concerned, when he left headquarters downtown, he drove up to Mulholland Drive. He was there for almost an hour, and then he came here. So how the hell could he kill your goddamn chemist? Anyway, I got cause to be pissed off, the two of you coming up here sore as hell because I got a cop on my force smart enough to figure out that something is going to happen!"

Bones started to say something, and Wainwright cut him off. "Also, I don't like nobody coming here and accusing one of my men. I'll match my force against any."

"Just a minute, before we say a lot of things we're going to regret. Nobody accused anyone. You asked us if we thought Masuto had killed him. You got to admit, it's goddamn strange. Also, what about this killing up on Mulholland? Your man Beckman practically gets into a fight with our cops—they shouldn't touch the body until Masuto gets there. Who the hell is Masuto? The boy was in Los Angeles, not in Beverly Hills, and your men come bulling in there and pushing us around."

Wainwright turned to Masuto. "What about it, Masao?"

Masuto spoke slowly and chose his words carefully. The last thing in the world he desired at this moment was a feud with the Los Angeles police. "Perhaps Beckman was assertive. It's the way he works. But he doesn't push people around, certainly not Los Angeles policemen. No one does. I think Captain Kennedy knows that. It's quite true that the boy's body was in

Los Angeles, but he wasn't killed there. His body was dumped out of a car. We think the boy was involved in a murder case, and the killer executed him to get rid of a witness."

"What murder case?"

Masuto spelled out the events of the day, detail for detail. When he had finished, there was a long moment of silence, and then Kennedy said, "And what about the chemist?"

"We are dealing here," Masuto said, "with a pure botulism toxin, not with decayed food, but with the toxin that the botulinus produces. Your man at the poison lab assured me that only a trained chemist could produce it. Well, what kind of a chemist would risk his freedom and career to produce a deadly poison—a poison which he would have to surmise would be used to kill people? What kind of a chemist would be vulnerable? Almost certainly a chemist mixed up in the dope rackets. The odds are that he would have a criminal record. My own guess is that we are dealing with a killer who is indifferent to human life and allows nothing to stand in his way. He gets rid of witnesses. That's why he killed the Chicano kid, so my analysis was not entirely fortuitous. I guessed that sooner or later he would kill the chemist. He tried the botulism, and it failed. Now, something else. Was the chemist killed with a twenty-two pistol?"

"That's right," Bones said grudgingly.

"Shot behind the ear?"

"Yes."

"No sound of the shot?"

"No, no sound of a shot," Kennedy said.

"Have you got anything?"

"Not a damn thing. The chemist's name is Leroy Kender. He served time for refining horse. Then he was picked up for angel dust, but that didn't stick. He lived alone in a furnished room on Sixth Street. He had almost nine hundred dollars in his pocket, so it wasn't robbery."

"It wasn't robbery," Masuto said. "This one doesn't touch the money in his victims' pockets."

"That's rich blood," Kennedy said.

"Very rich. Fingerprints?"

"We'll have plenty of fingerprints. But what the hell good are fingerprints unless you got something to match them with?" Kennedy asked.

"This one doesn't leave fingerprints. But you have something to match if you want it," Masuto said.

"What's that?"

"The bullet that killed the Chicano boy you found on Mulholland and the bullet that killed the chemist. I have a notion they'll match up."

"Okay," Kennedy said. "I'm glad you leveled with us, Masuto. Maybe we had a reason to be sore, maybe not. If you catch up with this killer—well, we got our own case against him."

"I'll stay in touch," Masuto said.

"And keep us informed," Wainwright said. "We're in this together."

When the two Los Angeles cops had left, Wainwright shook his head and said, "One day, Masao, you'll get us in deep, and I swear when you do I'll let you fry in your own juice. Where's Beckman?"

"Sitting in his car outside the Crombie place."

"On overtime."

"Yes." Then he added, "I have the four women there."

"Where?"

"In the Crombie house. I had Laura Crombie bring them over."

"Why?"

"Because I want to talk to them. Because someone is trying to kill them, and if it happens it won't do this city's image one bit of good."

"You really think someone's trying to kill four dames whose only crime is that they live in Beverly Hills?"

"He's killed three people already."

"I got to call my wife," Wainwright said.

Masuto went downstairs. He came out of the building and paused for a moment under the light of the entrance. He never heard the shot, only felt a hot pain at the side of his chin, as if a bee had stung him. As he put his hand up to his face, he heard the roar of a motor, and across the street a dark car shot away.

There was blood on his hand.

A prowl car had just parked, and the officer leaped out and ran over to him. "What happened, Sarge?"

"A bullet nicked me," Masuto said.

"I didn't hear a shot."

"He uses a silencer. Look around a bit, Cowley. See if you can find the bullet. A little slug, a twenty-two. It might be embedded in the door."

"I ought to get after him."

"We don't know who he is or where he went," Masuto said gently. "Look for the bullet." Then he went back into the building.

Wainwright was just putting down the phone. "What in hell happened to you?" he demanded.

"I have been shot."

"Let me look at it. Yeah, it just nicked your cheek. Where do they keep the peroxide?"

"In the john."

Wainwright swabbed out the cut and put a Band-Aid across it. "You say he was in his car across the street. That has got to be sixty feet, and with a twenty-two pistol, he is one hell of a shot, maybe an impossible shot."

"He could have had a shoulder brace or it could have been a target gun this time, maybe a rifle. Or maybe just laying the pistol on the door of his car to steady it. Or he might have been aiming for my chest."

"Which would still be pretty damn good shooting."

"It would."

"Why you?" Wainwright asked. "If it's the same guy?"

"It is."

"How can you be sure?"

"Because he called and spoke to Polly, and she told him I was handling the case."

"That's stupid!"

"No—he might have had information. How was she to know? I'm the one who's stupid. He knows a lot about us. Well, now I know something about him."

"What, if I may ask?"

"He—it—the killer is a man. He's an expert pistol shot. He drives a Mercedes."

"So do half the people in Beverly Hills. But why a Mercedes? You said you couldn't see the car, just that it was dark."

"I know that sound. There's a particular sound when you gun a Mercedes. Also, he's rich."

"Not uncommon in this town."

"And he has an enormous ego and a complicated but childish mind. The botulism, for example. Not brilliant, not even clever, but complicated. Also—and this I think is where I'll get him—he has killed before."

"You mean the chemist and the Chicano kid?"

"No—no. There's killing somewhere in his past that we don't know about."

As Masuto was leaving, Wainwright called after him, "Masao, be careful."

"I am always careful," Masuto said.

Chapter 6

ALICE GREENE

A curved drive in a half-moon shape swept in from the sidewalk, past the front door of Laura Crombie's house, and then back to the sidewalk. A low hedge of variegated plantings stretched parallel to the sidewalk, from one end of the driveway to the other. The house was well lit inside, but the driveway was in darkness.

Masuto parked his car in the street, behind Beckman's car, and then walked slowly up the driveway where three other cars were parked. At one side, the driveway was intersected by a connection with the garage. The garage doors were closed. Masuto looked closely at the three parked cars. The first in line was a Mercedes two-seater 450 SL. "Twenty-seven thousand dollars," Masuto said to himself. Beverly Hills was not a place where people hid their wealth under a bushel. Next, a Cadillac Seville, sixteen thousand dollars. The third in line was a Porsche Turbo Carrera, the price of which, Masuto guessed, ranged between forty and forty-five thousand dollars, just about twice what he and Kati had paid for their little house when they first purchased it. Well, he thought, his two children were safe at home in their beds and Kati was at a consciousness-raising session, while the four women inside the house were in deadly danger. He made no moral judgment, nor did he place value on a piece of shiny machinery priced at forty thousand dollars. Himself, he was paid to protect these people, and this he would do to the best of his ability.

Masuto rang the bell. Beckman opened the door for him. "Thank God you're here, Masao. You're five minutes late."

"You're counting?"

"You're damn right I am. These dames are driving me nuts." He spoke in a whisper.

"How's that?"

"They been drinking. I tried to lean on them and make them hold back, but they just don't listen."

"Are they drunk?"

"Not so you can notice, but they put down the stuff like it was going out of style."

"Where are they?"

"In what she calls the library."

"Let's go in."

He followed Beckman into the room. The four women sat facing each other, two on easy chairs, two on the couch. Each had a glass in her hand.

"Welcome, Oriental sleuth," Mrs. Crombie said. "Has the stalwart Beckman been telling you we are drunk? We are not—only nicely, warmly lit. Do you want a drink?"

"No, I don't want a drink."

"He's very handsome but severe. So severe. So straight," a pretty red-headed woman said. She was the youngest of the four, and Masuto guessed that this was Mitzie Fuller.

"Fuzz," a slender blonde said, shrugging. Alice Greene, Masuto decided.

The fourth, Nancy Legett, just stared at him. Her eyes were full of fear. She was small and dark. She was in one of the big easy chairs, not just sitting in it but giving the impression of being trapped there, trapped and doomed and afraid.

Masuto reacted to her. Her fragile, empty world of wealth and possession had come tumbling down around her head. As for the others, they could put on masks. She had no masks. He scarcely heard Laura Crombie introducing the women. For one long moment, he was in a state reached sometimes in his meditation, when he knew things that he did not otherwise know.

"The whole thing," said Alice Greene, "is a crock. A well-filled crock. I'm here because Laura pleaded with me to stay. Otherwise, I'd tell you to take your fantasy and stuff it. How dare you do this to us! This is Beverly Hills, not the South Bronx. As for this business of being in danger, another crock! That chocolate was not meant for me. It was delivered to the wrong house."

"Alice, for Christ's sake, shut up," Laura Crombie said.

"Give me another drink."

"No!"

"Then I'll get it myself."

"Like hell you will! This is my house!"

"Great. I'm glad you told me. Now I'm going to get the hell out of here!"

Both women were on their feet, and Laura said, "No—no, I'm sorry. Please. Please stay."

"Not on your life."

"Alice, I'm begging you."

"Peddle it somewhere else."

Laura turned to Masuto. "Stop her. Make her stay here."

Facing him, Alice Greene said, "Just try it, buster. Just lay one hand on me."

"I'm not going to lay a hand on you," Masuto said gently. "You are in danger, great danger. Believe me."

"I'll handle it. I've handled it for thirty-six years, mister. I'm all grown up. You might not think so to look at me, but I'm all grown up. Now get out of my way."

She pushed past him, and Laura pleaded, "Can't you stop her?"

"I have no right to stop her."

She ran after Alice Greene. Masuto and Beckman followed. Alice was fumbling with the locks on the door.

"How do you open this stupid thing?"

Laura Crombie stood back and whispered to Masuto, "She's in no condition to drive. Can't you arrest her for drunken driving?"

"Only if she commits a violation while driving," Beckman said.

Alice Greene finally opened the door and walked to her car with long steps. She got into the Mercedes and with the light on from the open car door, the two men and the woman in the doorway could see her fumbling in her purse for the car keys.

"Sy," Masuto said to Beckman, "get into your car and follow her. Anything—even a rolling stop at a stop sign—anything. The moment she steps out of line, pull her in for drunk driving."

At that moment, just as Beckman took off for his car, Alice slammed her car door, switched on her lights, and turned the ignition key. The explosion rocked the house and the burst of flame lit up the driveway. Laura screamed. Masuto and Beckman rushed toward the car and then were physically repelled by the curtain of heat.

"Call the fire department!" Masuto shouted at Laura Crombie.

He and Beckman circled the car, looking for some opening, and then Beckman pulled Masuto back. "Your eyebrows are singed, Masao. It's no use. She's dead."

"Why didn't I stop her? Why?"

"Because you didn't know."

People were beginning to come out of their houses, to stand watching. A prowl car pulled up, then a second one. In the distance the siren of a fire engine sounded.

"Get inside with the women," Masuto told Beckman. "Keep them in the house and keep the door closed. They'll be hysterical by now, so quiet them down."

People were crowding onto the driveway, and one of the uniformed policemen was ordering them back. The fire truck screamed its way into the street, and a moment later a fire hose opened up on the burning car.

"Twenty-seven grand for that heap," Masuto heard someone in the crowd say. Evidently no price was put on the human life. The uniformed officer who had come in the second prowl car said, "For Christ's sake, Sarge, what in hell goes on here?"

"Get on your radio and patch it through to downtown. I want the L.A. bomb squad up here, and tell them to bring their trunk."

"Okay."

"Are you in charge here?" a fireman asked Masuto. "We'd like to move those two cars," pointing to the Seville and the Porsche. "You got the keys?"

"Don't touch them. They may be wired. Can you get the woman out?"

The fire was out now, the car a blackened, smoking heap.

"We'll try. The ambulance will be here any minute. But she's dead. No question about that. That heat would kill her in ten seconds if the blast didn't."

Another police car with two more officers pulled up. "I want those people back in their houses," Masuto said to them. "There's nothing they can do and there's nothing for them to see."

"Who's in the car, Sarge?"

"A woman," Masuto said shortly. "Does that captain know about this?"

"They called him from the station. He'll be here any minute."

"Well, get those people back into their homes. If they ask, tell them it was an accident and that's all you know."

"That *is* all we know," one of the cops said.

The fireman had pried open the door of the smoking car, and Masuto walked over and forced himself to look at the charred figure that a few moments ago had been a vital, living woman. The metal of the Mercedes was still hot and the firemen were wetting it down with a soft stream of water. At that moment, the rescue ambulance arrived, and a moment later, Wainwright in his shirtsleeves.

"My God," one of the rescue men said, "that poor woman."

"Where shall we take her, Sarge?"

"Take her to the morgue at All Saints," Masuto said. "We don't need an autopsy. Tell them to hold the body until we inform the family."

Wainwright stood there in silence, his face glum and unhappy. From somewhere inside the house, Beckman remembered to switch on the driveway lights. The sudden blaze of illumination made the scene even more grotesque.

"It's over now," the fire captain told Masuto. "Do you want us to call the tow truck?"

"No, just leave it here. I've called the L.A. bomb squad."

The rescue people wrapped Alice Greene's body in a rubber sheet, put it on a stretcher and into the ambulance. The firemen climbed into their truck and drove off. By now, most of the curious had been ushered back into their houses or on their way. The uniformed cops stood around uncertainly, and Beckman came out of the house.

Still, Wainwright had not said a word.

"How are they?" Masuto asked Beckman.

"They got it under control. They were pretty hysterical at first, and I don't blame them. But we talked."

"No more booze?"

"I was hard about that," Beckman said.

"Go back and stay with them," Masuto told him. "Until I come in. Tell them I must talk to them tonight."

"How long?"

Masuto shrugged, and Beckman went back into the house.

"All right," Wainwright finally said, "tell me about it."

"I was talking to the women and she wouldn't have any of it."

"Who? I don't even know who."

"Alice Greene."

"The one who got the poisoned candy? The dog?"

"That's right. She had a few drinks and she said she was going home. I couldn't stop her."

"Did you try?" Wainwright asked.

"Short of using force. I didn't want her on the street and I didn't want her in her house. I told Beckman to follow her, and the moment she did anything that could be called a violation to pull her in for drunk driving. If I had dreamed that the car was wired—"

"We don't dream those things. What then?"

"She turned the key in the ignition, and the car blew."

"No chance to get her out?"

"In two seconds, the car was a ball of flame."

"Yes." Wainwright nodded at the Seville and the Porsche.

"Nancy Legett and Mitzie Fuller."

"They could be wired too."

"I thought of that. The men from the bomb squad can look at them. I don't know what's in her garage. That could be wired too. This murderous bastard we're dealing with doesn't do anything by halves. He's thorough."

"I want him, Masao," Wainwright said, "and I want him quick. We're a small town, and we can't have this. If the media start putting two and two together, they're going to tie this whole package in to Beverly Hills. We got four murders now. You say the other three women are inside?"

"That's right."

"I don't want anything to happen to them, Masao. If anything does, I am going to be one angry son of a bitch. I got enough to explain. They're going to come down on me like a ton of bricks over what happened here tonight."

"I'll do my best."

"You talk those women into spending the night

here. I'm going to leave two men here, one in front and one in back, and when the bomb squad people come, I want them to go through the basement of the house as well as the cars and the garage. God only knows what that lunatic is up to."

A few minutes after Wainwright left, the bomb squad arrived, their big armored truck grinding into the driveway. Kelp, the head of the squad, looked at the remains of the Mercedes and shook his head. "You hate to see it with a car like that." He had worked with Masuto before. "Anyone in it?" he asked.

"A lady."

"God help her."

"Those two cars might also be wired," Masuto said, pointing to the Seville and the Porsche.

"They're classy cars. Do you have the keys?"

"I'll get them for you."

"Do you want us to be careful of prints? Are you going to dust the cars?" Kelp asked.

Masuto shook his head. "Not with this one. He doesn't leave prints. What do you think it is?" nodding at the burned Mercedes.

"Just a guess. Dynamite and a detonator. She turned the ignition key and it blew, is that it?"

"That's it."

His men were already working on the burned car. "Dynamite," one of them called out.

"Does a job like that take skill?" Masuto asked.

"Nothing to it if you know something about cars. The explosive end of it is very primitive. Tie a few sticks of dynamite together and attach a detonator. Funny thing about dynamite. Blow a stick here on the driveway and it wouldn't even put a hole in it. Go off like a big firecracker. But confine it properly and it's a demon. The connection with the ignition is a little more complicated, but nothing I couldn't teach you in fifteen minutes."

"So it doesn't require an expert?"

"Not at all. But don't misunderstand me. There are experts in this business. Did she lock her car?"

"Not the doors."

"That makes it easier, because the hood release is usually inside. We'll go over the cars, Masao, but you'd better get me the keys."

"I'll do that. I also want you to look at the car in the garage and then check the basement."

"What in hell have you got going here?"

"I wish I knew."

"Well, it ain't the Beverly Hills I read about. We'll check out the place, Masao."

Then Masuto went into the house for the keys.

Chapter 7

THE WOMEN

It was eleven o'clock. The bomb squad had done its work and departed, discovering no other lethal contraptions. The car in Laura Crombie's garage and the two cars in the driveway were clean. The burned wreckage had been towed away, and a uniformed policeman was stationed in front of the house, with another at the back of the house. Masuto had left orders that the press and the television people, who were on the scene no more than twenty minutes after the incident occurred, should be told nothing, and they were barred from the house by the policeman on guard.

"Still," Beckman said to Masuto, "sooner or later you got to talk to them."

"I don't. Let Wainwright talk to them."

They were in the kitchen of the Crombie house, seated around the big kitchen table—Beckman, Masuto, Mitzie Fuller, Nancy Legett, and Laura Crombie. Laura Crombie had put up a large pot of coffee and sliced ham for sandwiches. Masuto and Beckman were both hungry. Mitzie Fuller, who said she couldn't even think of food, had two sandwiches. Only Nancy Legett did not eat. She was still struggling for composure, and every few minutes she would begin to weep silently. Laura was self-contained and practical. She had things to do. It was her house and these were her guests.

"Violence is new to you," Masuto said to them. "I hate violence as much as you do and I fear it too, but I live with it. My wife is made miserable by it, but she accepts it because it is my life. Tonight you must accept it, because if we are ever to find out who is doing this, we must talk calmly. I must ask you questions, and you must answer them sensibly."

"It's crazy," said Laura. "What kind of person am I? Instead of weeping for Alice, I keep thinking of all that glass in my driveway."

"That's understandable. It's less frightening, less awful. Your mind avoids the horror. Sy," he said to Beckman, "get a broom and sweep up that glass."

"Oh, no. No. I'll do it tomorrow," she protested.

"Glad to. Gives me something to do," Beckman said, relieved to be released from this well of emotion.

"Now all of you listen to me," Masuto said to the women. "We're in this together. He tried to kill me too." He touched the Band-Aid on his chin. "A long shot that missed."

"Oh, no!" Nancy Legett exclaimed.

"This crazy monster—what does he want?" Mitzie Fuller asked.

"That's what we're trying to find out, and perhaps we can right here. Let me spell out the sequence of events, so they'll be clear in your minds. Try to think clearly and objectively. I know how hard that is and I know what a disturbing day you've all had, but I want you to put that aside. You are thinking that it is impossible. It is not impossible. Mrs. Greene will not be helped by our indulgence, but she may be avenged by our objectivity."

"I'll try," Nancy said. "I know you mean me. I'll try."

"I mean all of you. Now let me trace what happened. A package of poisoned pastry was sent here. The man who sent it—"

"How do you know it was a man?" Mitzie interrupted.

"I know. Leave it at that. The man who sent it was intent upon killing one of you—not all of you—but one of you. Yes, it was to his benefit if more than one of you died, even if all of you died."

"I don't understand," said Laura.

"A very simple conclusion. Since all of you might have eaten the pastry, he was ready to accept all four murders. Or some of the four, since some of you might not have eaten. It was a scattershot thing. Even the death of one of you might have satisfied him."

"But why?"

Beckman returned to the room. "Quiet?" Masuto asked him. Beckman nodded. "Go through the house," Masuto said, "doors, windows—"

Beckman nodded and left the room.

"Why?" Masuto said. "Well, for one thing, he's insane. But perhaps all murderers are. And for another—well, let me reserve that for the time being."

"You don't think there's anyone—anyone hiding here?" Nancy asked.

"No, but it never hurts to be thorough. Let me go on. Ana Fortez ate the pastry and died. The Chicano boy who bought the pastry and who probably delivered it here was murdered on the same day. The chemist who prepared the poisonous toxin was murdered today." The fear in the eyes of the three women increased. "I don't like to tell you this,"

Masuto said, "but I must. You must know what kind of a man we are dealing with."

"Why must we know?" Nancy asked tremulously.

"Because I'm sure you know him. We'll hold that for a while. I want to ask you who killed Alice Greene."

They shook their heads in bewilderment.

"Guess," he urged them. "The most likely candidate. Who hated her enough to kill her?"

"No one."

"She's dead. Who hated her enough to kill her?"

"Her husband," Laura Crombie said softly.

"Is that what you mean by 'know him'?" Nancy Legett asked plaintively. "Do you mean that this monster is someone we know, someone we have spoken to?"

"Didn't you hear him?" Mitzie Fuller said shrilly, a note of hysteria in her voice. "He thinks Alice's husband is the killer."

"Her ex. Not her husband, her ex," Laura corrected her.

"No, I do not!" Masuto said sharply. "Will you please pay attention to what I am saying? Including Mrs. Greene, you are four divorced women. You have that in common. You are friends. You are attacked as a group. I must find a reason, a motive. I must know who has the need to destroy you. Mrs. Greene was killed. This does not mean her husband killed her. It also does not mean that he is innocent. We deal with him as a person under suspicion."

At that moment, the telephone rang, an explosive sound that startled all three women. There was a wall extension in the kitchen, and Laura Crombie picked it up.

"Alan," she said. Pause. "Yes, it's true. It's terrible—too terrible to believe." Pause. "No, we don't know why. The whole thing is like a nightmare." Pause. "I tell you I don't know any more than that. She turned the ignition key, and the whole car went up in flames. It was awful. She never had a chance." Pause. "Yes, the police were here. I believe Sergeant Masuto is in charge of the case." She looked at Masuto.

"I'll talk to him," Masuto said.

"He's here, if you wish to talk with him." She handed Masuto the telephone.

The voice was crisp and businesslike, yet Masuto felt he could detect an undercurrent of emotion and uncertainty. "This is Alan Greene. I was married to Mrs. Greene."

"This is Sergeant Masuto. I'm in charge of the case."

"Can you tell me what happened?"

"No more than Mrs. Crombie told you."

"There's a damn sight more than that."

"All right. Suppose you come over to headquarters tomorrow at ten A.M."

Hesitation, then, "Okay, I'll be there. Meanwhile, where have they taken Alice's body?"

"To the morgue at All Saints Hospital. Could you notify her next of kin?"

"The only kin I know about is a brother in New Orleans. They haven't seen each other in years. I don't think the son of a bitch would lift his ass unless he's in her will. I'll take care of the funeral arrangements."

"Talk of the devil," Mitzie said as Masuto sat down at the kitchen table again.

"He said he'll take care of the funeral arrangements," Masuto said again.

"Alan's all heart," Laura said.

"And you think he hated her enough to kill her?"

"You never think in those terms, do you?" Laura Crombie replied. "He was paying her five thousand a month, but he could afford it. Would he kill her? He knew she'd never marry Monte and let him off the hook."

"Monte Sweet?"

"Yes. The comic."

"Where is he now?"

"He was in Vegas."

"Do you know when? Is he still there?"

"If you're thinking of Monte as a suspect, forget it. He couldn't kill a fly. Anyway, she showered him with gifts."

"What about her will?" Mitzie said. "Who else would she leave it to? That house of hers has to be worth half a million."

"Mrs. Fuller," Masuto said to Mitzie, "who would want to kill you?"

Oddly enough, she began to giggle. "I'm sorry, I'm sorry," she apologized. Masuto found her enchanting, and silently called himself to order. He enjoyed beautiful women. They disturbed his objectivity, and Mitzie Fuller was very beautiful—orange-colored hair that did not come out of a bottle, large blue eyes, and a round figure that was five pounds short of being plump. "I don't know why I'm doing this, but your question—"

"I asked it."

"I never thought of myself that way. Who does? Who ever says to herself, I'm being set up for a murder? Well, sure, Billy Fuller would like to kill me. If he could get away with it. If it wouldn't interfere with his career. If it could be written into his contract. In fact, he specified the act. But who doesn't? I mean married, who doesn't?"

"I'm not sure I know what you do mean," Masuto said.

"Well, you know how it is. No, maybe you don't. Maybe the Japanese don't operate that way."

"What way?"

"You know—you bitch, I'm going to kill you."

"You're telling me that's what your husband said to you?"

"But it doesn't mean anything. First of all, I made the number one mistake that any woman can make. I married a film director. That's a very special kind of guy. You know, Sergeant, your sex is nothing to write home about, even under the best of circumstances, but if you were to list types of men from A to Z, with A being the very rare nice guy, Z would have to be a film director. They are power-ridden little tin gods—"

"Oh, come on," Nancy Legett interrupted her. "I've known decent directors. Some of them are pussy-cats."

"But seriously, does your husband hate you enough to kill you?" Masuto asked.

"Yes," she said, flatly and bleakly. The laughter was gone.

"Why?"

Her lips came together and tightened. Masuto waited.

"His hatred," she said finally, "is a personal matter that I don't intend to talk about. And it's not the lousy alimony he pays. He took on a picture for seven hundred thousand dollars, and after a month of pre-production, the producers found him so obnoxious they paid him four hundred thousand to break his contract. So the money's nothing."

"Was he in the army?"

"The navy. He's a lieutenant in the naval reserve."

"And where is he working now?"

"They tell me he's doing a film at Metro. I couldn't care less."

"And what about you, Mrs. Legett?" Masuto asked, turning to Nancy. "Who would want to kill you?"

"That's a terrible thing to ask me."

"But I must," Masuto said softly.

"Why should anyone want to kill me? I've never hurt anyone. I never hurt my husband. Even when he told me he was leaving me, I didn't make it hard for him. I knew he had stopped loving me long ago. Perhaps I had stopped loving him too. I don't know. And I don't have any lovers to make him jealous or angry. Look at me. Do I look like a woman who has lovers?"

She began to sob, and Laura Crombie put her arm around her and said to Masuto, "Must you, tonight? We're all tired and frightened."

"I'm afraid I must. Please, try to pull yourself together, Mrs. Legett. I promise you, there will be no more danger, no more hurt and fear—but only if you help me. You must help me."

"I'll try."

"You don't feel that your ex-husband hates you?"

"No."

"That's no good, Nancy," Laura told her. "You have to tell him the truth. Otherwise we'll never get to the bottom of this."

"Why should he hate me? It's four months since he made any support payments. I don't dun him. I pay for the children's support. I don't ask anything of him."

"Nancy!"

She sighed and nodded.

"Enough to kill you?" Masuto pressed her.

"No!" she snapped.

"All right," said Laura Crombie. "You won't, I will. Fulton Legett is a cold-blooded bastard. He has ice in his veins. His children do not like him, and for that he blames Nancy—"

"Laura, stop," Nancy pleaded.

"No, I will not stop. Someone has to tell Sergeant Masuto, and you won't. Nancy wanted the divorce, because that bastard was destroying her. Cutting her to pieces, putting her down every time she opened her mouth, and do you know why? Because she has more brains in her little finger than he has in that stupid skull of his."

"Please stop," Nancy begged her.

"No, I will not stop. This isn't gossip. We've just seen Alice murdered, and we're sitting here fighting for our lives." She faced Masuto. "He became a producer because Nancy made him one. That was twenty years ago. Nancy found a delightful story, emptied her own personal bank account to option it, and then talked Paramount Pictures into putting up the money to develop it and accepting Fulton Legett as the producer. That was a hit and his next three pictures were hits because Nancy chose them and supervised, even while she was pregnant. She still owns half of his company, and they have an agreement whereby if one dies, the other inherits."

"Laura, how could you!" Nancy burst out. "You're practically accusing Fulton of being behind this whole thing, of killing Alice and three other people. Why would he?"

"I don't know why he would want to kill me," Mitzie said. "He keeps calling and trying to take me out. I hate to say this, Nancy, but he does have the reputation of being bad news."

"You never told me," Nancy said.

"Why bug you? You're out of it and I have no intention of getting into it."

"How do you happen to know him?" Masuto asked Mitzie. "I understood that you and Mrs. Crombie met only a few weeks ago."

"He knows Billy, my own ex. He's been after Billy to do a film for him, but Billy follows the money and right now Fulton Legett is broke. I don't know how much you know about the film business, Sergeant, but the game is played like a jigsaw puzzle. If you can get a top-flight director and put him together with an important star and an important property, which is what they call a book in this business, a property, you're well on your way to getting a studio to finance a film. That's why Fulton Legett has been nosing around my Billy."

Masuto nodded, and asked Nancy Legett, "Was your husband in the army, Mrs. Legett?"

"Yes. He was in Korea."

"In the infantry?"

"No, he was an airplane mechanic."

"Why are you so certain," Laura Crombie asked Masuto, "that one of our ex-husbands is the man you are looking for?"

"I'm not certain. But whoever the killer is, he links the four of you together. Apparently, he knows all of you, what your tastes are, what your habits are. Now tell me, do you know William Fuller, the director?"

She hesitated just a moment. "Yes, I do."

"Do you know Monte Sweet?"

"No, not personally. I never met him."

"Do you know Monte Sweet?" he asked Nancy Legett.

She shook her head.

He turned to Mitzie Fuller.

She smiled and shook her head. "No, not really."

"What does that mean, not really?" Masuto asked.

"You're worse than my analyst," Mitzie said. "It means just that—not really."

He turned back to Laura Crombie. "We have three women whose ex-husbands have motives, if not for murder at least for hatred. What about your ex-husband, Mrs. Crombie?"

She shrugged. "Since this is naked time, I'll let down my hair with the rest. When I married Arthur Crombie three years ago, he didn't have a red penny. I'm a very wealthy woman. Even then, I was not poor. I put Arthur into the real estate business. Oh, he isn't stupid. He's damn smart, but he just loused up everything he touched. This time, for some reason, it was different. He got into it just as property values out here began to skyrocket. He had been a real estate agent before, so he knew the ropes, and he specialized in very expensive homes. Today he has one of the hottest businesses in town. Then, six months after we were married, my father died. I was the only heir, and the estate came to something over seven million. Arthur got his share of that, since it was I who was pleading for the divorce, not him. In other words, today Arthur is a millionaire because the lady you are looking at is a damn fool. Murder me? He ought to erect a monument to me."

Masuto nodded and waited.

"That's it."

"Do you have any children, Mrs. Crombie?"

"No!" hard and short.

Nancy Legett was staring at her. Masuto watched her, then looked at Laura.

Beckman came back into the kitchen. Masuto guessed that he had searched every corner of the house. Beckman would do it that way. He looked at Beckman, and Beckman said softly, "Okay."

Masuto waited. Finally, she said, "Yes. I told you. But what difference does it make? How does it come into this?"

"I don't know. I don't know how anything comes into this. I'm trying to find out."

"I had a daughter," Laura said bleakly. "She's dead. I told you that this morning."

"Please tell me about it."

"Why?"

"Because I'm trying to save lives."

"She's dead. It has nothing to do with this."

"I don't want to go elsewhere and pick up shreds of gossip. I want you to tell me."

"There's nothing to tell. My daughter was killed in an automobile accident. Have you ever lost a child, Sergeant Masuto? Would you find it amusing to discuss?" With that, she leaped to her feet and strode out of the room.

"She can't talk about it," Nancy Legett said to him. "It was over three years ago, and it doesn't get any better. Kelly was a beautiful, wonderful child."

"Kelly?"

"They called her Kelly. Her real name was Catherine. Laura lived for the child—especially after Laura's first husband died. We don't all make rotten marriages. Laura's first marriage was a good one," Nancy said.

"Do you know whether Arthur Crombie was in the army?"

"Yes, he was a pilot in Korea. He still flies. He has his own plane now."

"And did you know Arthur Crombie?" Masuto asked Mitzie.

"Yes—not too well. About a week ago, he called me and then came to my house."

"Why?"

"You know what's going on in the real estate market here in California. It's even worse in Beverly Hills. The moment words gets around that you might want to sell your house they descend on you like scavengers. Crombie heard that I wanted to sell my house, and he came by to look at it."

"And do you want to sell it?"

"I think so. It's a huge barn of a place on Palm Drive, and it makes no sense for me to go on living there. My life with Fuller was quick and merry. We were married only six months. Things still aren't settled. As soon as they are, I'll sell the house."

"And when he was there, did anything out of the way happen? Anything he might have asked you?"

"About my house?"

"About anything."

She shook her head. "No. Nothing unusual. Just the general questions—you know, how is the plumbing and does the roof leak and that sort of thing. It's an old house, a big Spanish Colonial, so it's far from perfect."

"And that's the only time you saw Arthur Crombie?"

Did she hesitate? Was there something in her large blue eyes? If it was there, it was gone instantly. She was an amazing self-controlled young woman, Masuto decided.

"Yes. The only time."

Laura Crombie returned to the room. "I'm sorry,"

she said to Masuto. "I behaved like an emotional fool. But this has been a terrible day, Sergeant."

"I know that."

"There are pains that go away. The loss of a child is not one of them," she said.

"I know that too."

"How long are you going to keep us here in this house?"

"I'm not keeping you here. I have no authority to keep you here. I suggest very strongly that the three of you spend the night here, and that no one leave the house tomorrow until I see you."

"And when will that be?"

"Some time tomorrow afternoon, I hope."

"I have a luncheon date and a hairdresser appointment," Mitzie Fuller said, "not to mention a date that I broke tonight and put off until tomorrow."

"I hope you'll be able to keep your date. I suggest you cancel the luncheon and the hairdresser appointment."

"Who's going to scragg me at Tony Cooper's?"

"Stop it, Mitzie," Nancy said. "He's deadly serious."

"Can you put up Detective Beckman? I want him to stay here tonight."

"If I have to give him my own bed," Laura said. "Right now, the only men in the world who interest me are oversized policemen. But must I have that uniformed policeman standing outside my door?"

"He'll leave," Masuto told her. "Detective Beckman can take care of anything that might come up."

Beckman walked with him to the front door. "Well?" he asked.

"It takes shape. Not too clearly, but at least it begins to take on some shape," Masuto said.

"You wouldn't like to tell me about it? Because for me it don't have any shape at all."

"Not yet."

"The house is wired with an alarm system," Beckman said. "The downstairs windows are locked. For that matter, so are those upstairs. The place is air conditioned. You don't mind if I get some sleep?"

"Not at all."

"You're all heart, Masao. When can I leave this place?"

"Some time tomorrow."

"When?"

"When I've picked up that murderous bastard."

Chapter 8

THE ZEN MASTER

It was just past one o'clock in the morning when Masuto pulled his car into the driveway of his house in Culver City. He closed the car door softly and turned the key in the lock of the kitchen door just as softly. The light was on in the kitchen, and on the kitchen table a note that said, "If you are hungry, there are things in the refrigerator." It was neither a friendly nor an unfriendly note. There was no greeting and no word of affection.

As quietly as he had entered the house, Masuto undressed in the bathroom, and then he slid into bed next to Kati, who appeared to be asleep. One session had apparently changed her. On other nights, she would somehow have managed to remain awake and have a hot drink and hot food waiting for him. Tonight, nothing.

He stretched out in bed and was just beginning to drift off when the sleeping Kati said, "Were they pretty?"

"Who?"

"The four women you spent the evening with."

"There were only three," he told her unfeelingly. "One was killed."

"Oh, no!"

"I'm sorry, Kati. It happened." He regretted that

he had flung this at her. There was no reason to tell her.

"Oh, I'm so sorry. And I was so angry at you."

"Why?"

"Not really angry. Only because I'm aware of the inequality of things."

"Yes. The consciousness-raising session."

"You told me to go."

"Oh, yes. Yes. I wanted you to go." He was very sleepy.

"I heard a lecture by Sono Akio."

"Yes."

"And Marta Suzuki. Not your Zen Suzuki. They are not even related. I asked."

"Yes, I'm sure you did."

"They both spoke about the condition of women in Japan. We think of Japan as a modern industrial country, but the women are still enslaved there. They have no rights and no equality."

"We don't live in Japan," Masuto muttered. "We live in California."

"You are not even interested. There is your basic, beginning point of it all. The man has no interest in what the woman thinks or does. But she, on the other hand, is supposed to exist in a condition of total interest in what he does."

Masuto sat up and stared at his wife in the darkness. "Kati dear—in one evening?"

"There is another meeting on Thursday. If you forbid me to go, things will be very unpleasant for both of us."

"I would not dream of forbidding you to go. What right have I to forbid you to do anything?"

"None," Kati said smugly.

Nevertheless, although Masuto awakened at six-thirty, Kati was already up and in the kitchen, dressed in her white and yellow kimono, looking very lovely and preparing breakfast. Masuto kissed her on the back of the neck, just below the thick knot of her black hair.

"Will you have eggs?" she asked him.

"Nothing this morning. I must go to the zendo this morning and meditate with Roshi Hakuin. I have some questions, and possibly he will be kind enough to answer."

"The children are still asleep. How can you leave without seeing the children? I am sure they've forgotten that they have a father."

"Then you must remind them."

"Masao, I'm so afraid. You walk with death always. If it reaches out and touches you—"

"Nothing will happen to me, Kati."

"Then why is there a bandage on your chin? What happened?"

"Just a scratch. It's nothing." He kissed her again. "I must go."

It was almost seven o'clock, yet he could not leave without looking at his roses, without walking once through the rose garden. Next to his wife, his children, and meditation, the roses were the most precious part of Masuto's life. A month before, he had received a rooted cutting of an old-fashioned cabbage rose from a distant relative in New Jersey, with a promise that the blooms would be six inches across. The first buds had just appeared. He wanted to dust them, but they were still wet with the morning dew, and reluctantly he left them.

The zendo was in downtown Los Angeles. At this hour, the streets would be quicker than the freeway, and Masuto drove down Pico Boulevard to Normandie Avenue. The zendo was a cluster of old wooden buildings that the students of the roshi had purchased and reconditioned. About forty families lived in the cluster that comprised the zendo, husbands, wives, and children—a kind of communal development that existed only in Los Angeles.

Masuto parked his car and walked to the meditation room, a long room with a polished wooden floor and two rows of pillows and mats. The room was actually two rooms joined together, the windows replaced by Victorian stained glass, picked up at auctions and flea markets. Roshi Hakuin sat at the far end of the room, a small, elderly Japanese man in a saffron-colored robe, sitting cross-legged, his eyes on the floor, while on either side, stretching down both sides of the room, sitting cross-legged on the pillows, were about twenty men and women in their morning meditation. One was a Burmese, two were Korean; the rest were Caucasian.

The room was filled with a soft, gentle morning light that diffused through the stained glass windows.

Masuto removed his shoes. He was about to take off his jacket when he realized that if he did, his revolver would be revealed. A zendo was no place to enter with a visible revolver. It was bad enough to enter with a concealed weapon. So he kept his jacket on, walked in his stocking feet to the unoccupied pillow closest to the roshi, sat down cross-legged, and began his meditation.

One by one, the others completed their meditation and left. Presently, only Masuto and the old Japanese master remained in the zendo. The roshi had finished meditating and was watching Masuto. Masuto put his palms together reverently, bowed his head, and waited.

"Welcome," Hakuin said, speaking in Japanese. He was never one to waste words.

"Thank you, Roshi, so grateful," Masuto replied, also in Japanese.

"For what?"

"For the privilege of speaking to you, Roshi."

"What nonsense! Since when is it a privilege to speak to a foolish old man? You would do better to tend your roses. That is what you tend, isn't it? Roses?"

"Yes, Roshi. But I am deeply troubled. I am in pursuit of a killer who has killed many times."

"Is that why you come into the zendo with a gun under your coat?"

"I'm sorry, so very sorry. But what was I to do once I was here?"

"And what have I to do with killers and killing, Masao?"

"What turns a man into a murderer?"

"Fear."

"But we are all afraid."

"And we are all murderers."

"This man," Masuto said, "is like a thousand other men. He has money and position and respect. But he kills again and again. I am trying desperately to understand before I act."

"Do you know who he is?" the Roshi asked.

"Yes—if I know why."

"A long time ago," the little old man said, "a young man came to a worthy roshi, and he said to him, Master, my father begs that I study Zen, but why? Tell me why. And this roshi, Masao, having more patience than I have, said to the young man, 'If you study Zen, you will not be afraid to die.' "

"I have heard the story many times. It puzzles me."

"Because you are stupid, Masao."

Masuto nodded.

"What else? You are part of a large police force, but you come to a foolish old Japanese man for an answer to your problem. This is certainly a very stupid thing to do. Anyway, as you already told me, you know who this man is. And I have told you why he does what he does."

The roshi rose and Masuto rose. They bowed to each other. The old man went to Masuto and put an arm around him.

"You are a good boy, Masao. Meditate more."

"If I could only find the time."

"Stand still and very quietly. The time will find you."

Chapter 9

ALAN GREENE

At headquarters, Masuto paused and listened. Fredericks, a uniformed cop, was leaving, and Masuto asked him, "Who's in there?"

"Wainwright, the city manager, and the mayor. They've been at it since eight-thirty."

The mayor was an unsalaried position. Like the president of the lodge who was the butt of everyone's anger, he did it for the "honor."

"There is no police force in the world," Wainwright was saying, his voice clear through the thin door, "that can prevent crime. I got a forty-page report from the F.B.I., if you want to read it. There's just no way we could have anticipated what happened to Mrs. Greene."

"As I understand, there were two policemen on the scene." That was the city manager.

"There could have been ten cops on the scene. How would they know that the car was wired? You don't look for a wired car in Beverly Hills."

"All right. That happened." The mayor's voice. "But the rumor's out that three other murders are tied into this."

A long silence.

"Well, for Christ's sake, yes or no?"

"Yes," Wainwright said shortly.

"What did you say? Yes?"

"Yes."

"Jesus God, four lousy murders! We're not that big. Don't you understand? We're just not that big."

"If it's any consolation," Wainwright said, "three of them took place outside the Beverly Hills city limits. So technically, those three belong to the Los Angeles cops."

"Well, who tied them in?"

"Masuto."

"Why?" the mayor cried. "For Christ's sake, why? What's the motive?"

"Because that's the way it is. If it's that way, that's the way it is," Wainwright said.

"What do you mean, that's the way it is. You just told us the way it is. Los Angeles has these killings," the mayor said.

"We got them too."

Masuto stopped listening and went into his office. It was a quarter after nine in the morning now. The Los Angeles *Times* had cleared space on the front page for the death of Alice Greene. It was mostly a picture of the burned car with only a few words of background squeezed in at the last moment. They specified that the two-seater Mercedes was priced at twenty-seven thousand dollars. It was almost obligatory to include a price in any Beverly Hills story. The deaths of the Chicano boy and the chemist rated only a few lines on inside pages. Violent death was hardly a novelty, unless of course it occurred in Beverly Hills inside a Mercedes.

Masuto dialed the number of the Crombie house. Mrs. Crombie answered.

"Our handsome Oriental jailer," she said. "When do we get sprung?"

"Soon, I hope. May I talk to Detective Beckman?"

"He's at breakfast."

"See if he can tear himself away."

"Hold on. He's finishing his second order of scrambled eggs and waffles and honey. I'll let him take it in the library where he'll have some privacy."

A minute or so later, Beckman's voice came over the phone, thickened by the fact that he was still chewing. "Do you know, Masao," he said, "those Arabs got something. Living with three women has its points."

"I'm sure. Anything happen?"

"Not a thing."

"How are the ladies?"

"A lot calmer. I can't say the same for my wife. You got to talk to her, Masao. She's sore as hell at me. All she had to hear is that I'm spending the night in a house with three Beverly Hills divorcées and she let go at me like God knows what I was up to. Like I'm doing this for fun."

"Aren't you?"

"Come on. You know better than that."

"All right, Sy. Now listen to me. You've been in that house for quite a while. In and out of every room, right?"

"Right."

"Now think. Mrs. Crombie had a daughter. Did you see the girl's picture anywhere?"

After a long moment of silence, Beckman said, "I wasn't looking for it, Masao. Maybe I saw it and paid it no mind."

"Just think for a while, Sy."

He thought about it. "I just can't remember. Like I said, I wasn't looking for it."

"All right. I want you to look for it. No questions

and don't give any hint of what you're looking for. Just let them know that your instructions are to keep checking out the house."

"And if I find it, what do you want me to do, pinch it?"

"No, no, no. Absolutely not. If you find a picture of the girl, just leave it alone. Don't touch it. Also, I want you to find out what the name of Mrs. Crombie's first husband was. Do it in a casual way. Nancy Legett would know. If you're alone with her, you might just ask as a matter of curiosity."

"Got it. You'll call back?"

"Within the hour."

Masuto put down the telephone and stared at the newspaper on his desk. He turned over in his mind what Roshi Hakuin had said to him. The trouble with putting questions to a Zen master was that the answers were always too simple. Complex answers to questions are always easy to understand. Simple answers are impossible to understand. Many, many years ago, this same Roshi Hakuin had given Masuto the ten pictures of the cow, ten very simple pictures of a little boy and a cow. "Look at them and when you know what they mean, come to me and tell me." It was five years before Masuto was able to answer correctly.

Now he did not have five years, or even five days. The madman he was dealing with would not be deterred by Detective Beckman and the locked doors of a house—given the supposition that he could keep the women in the house for even another day. An unwillingness to believe in impending danger is a very human quality. Otherwise, Masuto reflected, why would we all be so willing to live here in California on top of a whole network of earthquake faults?

Then he looked up and through the glass upper half of his office door, he saw the man. That would be Alan Greene, a tall, heavy-set, fleshy man of about fifty, gray hair set in a twenty-five-dollar hairdo, a fifty-dollar silk shirt, a thirty-dollar tie, and above it a wide, heavy chin, a tight mouth, and cold blue eyes. Masuto rose and opened the door for him.

"I'm Alan Greene," he said, regarding Masuto curiously. They always regarded him curiously on the first meeting, and while they looked at him, the question in their minds was, What is a Jap doing on the police force here? But except occasionally, it remained unspoken.

"I'm Detective Sergeant Masuto."

"Yeah. They told me outside you're in charge of this case."

"Why don't you sit down, Mr. Greene?"

He seated himself reluctantly, as if he were giving up an advantage. "What the hell goes on here?" he demanded suddenly. "You know the whole damn thing has to be a mistake. Nobody had any reason to kill Alice—except me."

"Except you?"

"Don't look at me like that, Sergeant. What you're thinking is pure bullshit."

"How do you know what I'm thinking?"

"I just told you that I'm the only one who had any reason to kill my ex-wife."

"Did you kill her?"

"If I had, you can be sure of one thing."

"What's that?"

"I would have strangled her with my bare hands."

"I see." Masuto nodded. "So you feel that it's the manner of her death that exonerates you."

"Jesus Christ, what in hell gives with you? You don't seriously think that I murdered my wife?"

"You just said—"

"Yeah, yeah," he interrupted. "And if you were married to that broad, you'd say the same thing. Would I kill her? If I had a dollar for every time I thought of breaking her neck, it would add up to enough to buy this crummy police station of yours. Do you know what I paid her? Five thousand dollars a month, not to mention what she collected under that beautiful law of ours called the Community Property Act. She could have paid me five grand a month and never missed it. She's been shacked up with Monte Sweet, not just for the year we've been divorced but for five years before that, and you are looking at the number one sucker in the world who was the last one to know. Everyone else knew it, everyone. Not me. So you ask me, would I kill her? In spades. But mister, I am not connected with the Mafia. I never have been. Monte Sweet is. Monte Seteloni. That, my friend, is his real name."

"Why the Mafia?" Masuto asked him.

"Because what happened last night was a Mafia killing. Who else wires cars?"

"It's not terribly complex. Could you, Mr. Greene?"

"Could I what?"

"Could you wire a car to explode when the ignition key is turned?"

"You're barking up the wrong tree. You know, I don't know why I'm sitting here at all, answering these stupid questions. I don't have to. I don't have to answer one goddamn question."

"No," Masuto said, smiling slightly, "you don't. You can get up and walk out of here right now. But I want to bring in the man who murdered your wife, and I will. If it's you, I'll bring you in. If it's someone else, I'll bring him in. Perhaps you want to help."

For almost a minute, Greene sat in silence, staring at Masuto, Finally, he said quietly, "Tell you something, Sergeant. If she had come to me, say yesterday, the day before, and she says to me, Al, let's give it another shot—if she did that, I don't know what I would have done. I was so goddamn crazy about that woman it drove me up the wall. I'm not saying I would have gone back into it. You got to be demented to keep putting your hand in a meat grinder. But that was the way I felt about her. Sure, I wanted to kill her. But I didn't."

"And the car?"

"Do you know what that little two-seater Mercedes cost? Twenty-seven big ones, and every nickel of it my money. Like I said, I would have strangled her. I wouldn't have smashed up the damn car."

"I asked whether you could have wired it."

"You're persistent, aren't you? You'd find out. I was in the engineers in Korea. You're damn right I could have wired it."

Masuto regarded him with new respect. This was a cool, calculating man, totally in command of himself. If he were the killer, the line he was taking was the best he could take. Admit motive. Admit desire. Admit ability. Leave no skeletons to fall out of closets when the doors were opened.

"Do you own a pistol, Mr. Greene?" Masuto asked him.

"I do. And I have a permit for it."

"What caliber?"

"Twenty-two."

"I see. A heavy gun, one that takes longs?"

"I don't know what you're getting at, Sergeant. Alice was not shot. She was killed in a car explosion. What the devil has that got to do with pistols?"

"There's a connection. I'd rather not go into it right now. But as you pointed out before, you don't have to answer any questions."

"I got nothing to hide."

"Then you're a fortunate man. I asked you about the pistol."

"It's a Browning automatic target gun. I use longs, that's right. I belong to the Beverly Hills Pistol Society, although I don't get to the range as often as I would like to."

"Are you a good shot?"

"I could put a bullet through your head at thirty yards," he said, smiling—his mouth smiling while his eyes remained cold and fixed on Masuto.

"I hope the occasion will not arise."

"I don't shoot people, only targets, Sergeant. And now if you're through investigating my own talents as a killer, I would like to get down to the subject at hand. Why was Alice murdered?"

"I was hoping you would tell me."

"You got to be kidding."

"You lived with her for ten years. Who would want to kill her?"

"We been through that."

"What about Monte Sweet?"

"Now wouldn't it make more sense to talk to him than to waste your time with me? He's got Mafia connections, and Alice's death was obviously a contract job. I'll tell you something else. My ex-wife's estate has to be worth better than a million. A lot better. Have you seen her house on Roxbury Drive?"

Masuto shook his head.

"I paid three hundred and twenty thousand for that house in nineteen seventy. She's been offered a million for it."

"How do you know? Did she tell you?"

"Arthur Crombie told me."

"Ah so." It escaped from him involuntarily. "Are you and Mr. Crombie friends?"

"We belong to the same golf club and—" He let that go.

"Were you going to say the same gun club?"

He stood up. "You know, Masuto, I don't like what's going on here. You want to talk to me about pistols, then I want to know why."

Masuto sighed and shrugged. "I'm trying to get to the bottom of something, that's all. You were saying that Mr. Crombie had a customer who was willing to pay a million dollars for your wife's house."

Standing there, Greene hesitated. Finally, he said, "I wish I knew what in hell you're after."

"A killer."

"What the devil has her house got to do with that?"

"You brought up the question of the house."

"Right. I did. Actually, the offer was one million two hundred thousand. That's not as crazy as it sounds, not in Beverly Hills. The house has seven bedrooms, a tennis court, and a swimming pool. An Iranian or an Arab made the offer, according to Crombie. I loved that house, and now it's gone. Do you wonder that I'd like to kill that broad?"

"Gone? Has it been sold?"

"What in hell's the difference? You don't think I'm in her will?"

"Who is in her will?"

"I'll give you long odds that every nickel she had goes to Monte Sweet."

"You never had children?"

"One miscarriage. She'd never take a chance again."

"Who are her lawyers?"

"Kellog and Cohen. They're in Westwood, I think."

Masuto scribbled down the names.

"Whoever did it," Greene said, "find the bastard."

"Yes, I intend to," Masuto said. "Meanwhile, I trust you won't be leaving town for the next few days."

Greene stared at Masuto for a long moment; then he nodded and left. Masuto dialed Information and got the telephone number for Kellog and Cohen. When he dialed that number, the woman's voice at the other end asked who he would like to speak to.

"Mr. Kellog."

She made the connection, and after a moment a man's voice told him that it was Kellog.

"This is Detective Sergeant Masuto of the Beverly Hills Police Department. I'm calling you concerning the death of Alice Greene, who, I understand, was a client of yours."

"Yes. What can I do for you?"

"I suggest you get our number from Information and call me back. In that way, you can be certain the call is valid."

"Masuto?"

"That's right."

He put down the phone and waited. A minute or so later, it rang. "What's all this about?" Kellog asked him.

"Your firm drew up Mrs. Greene's will. I would like to know who the beneficiary is under that will."

"Now you know I can't do that, Sergeant Masuto. This is a confidential matter between my client and myself."

"Your client is dead."

"That changes nothing. When the will is read, the beneficiary will become public. Until then, I must protect my client's confidentiality."

Masuto's voice hardened. "Your client, Mr. Kellog, is not only dead. She was savagely murdered. Her death was hideous and painful. I am engaged in an investigation of her death, in an effort to find the murderer. If you persist in your attitude, which constitutes interference with my investigation, I shall have to get a court order to examine that will. You know that I can get such an order. Wouldn't it be much simpler for you to name the beneficiary? Time is important."

There was a long silence, and then Kellog said, "Well—since you put it that way—I can't see that it will do any great harm."

"Thank you."

"Actually, there are three beneficiaries—the Bowdow Home, the Happy Bark Cemetery, and the Wolf Society."

Masuto was scribbling furiously. "Would you repeat the second one?"

Kellog went through the names again.

"And what exactly are these places?"

"The Bowdow Home is a hospital for dogs and cats, out in the Valley. The Happy Bark Cemetery is, as you might infer, a cemetery for well-loved pets. The Wolf Society—well, that's a bit more complicated. Not only do they carry out a whole program of anti-vivisectionist propaganda, but they are also in the vanguard of the wolf-jackal investigation and controversy."

"And what might that be?" Masuto asked.

"As I understand it, there is a theory that the husky, the chow, the Pekinese, and a few other breeds of dogs are descended from the wolf, while all other dogs are derived from the jackal. Mrs. Greene explained this to me at some length, but it remains rather fuzzy in my mind. In any case, the Wolf Society devotes itself to serious work on this theory."

Masuto took a deep breath and asked, "Are there no other beneficiaries?"

"None."

"Can you tell me the size of the estate?"

"That will have to be determined in probate, but I should guess it will amount to at least a million and a half—that is, including the property."

Masuto thanked him and put down the phone. Wainwright came into his office, and Masuto said, "Has it ever occurred to you that only huskies, chows, and Pekinese dogs are descended from wolves? I would have said the Pekinese evolved from a hamster, but that shows how much I know."

"What in hell are you talking about?"

"Alice Greene's will. A million and a half. It goes to dogs and cats."

"And where does that get us?"

"Nowhere. Precisely nowhere."

"I been with the city manager and the mayor, Masao. They want my scalp. Maybe they took it with them already. It's twelve hours since a murder took place in Beverly Hills, and we haven't tied up the case. It doesn't matter that the L.A.P.D. with seven thousand men on the force can't solve the Hillside

Strangler killings, to which they have assigned more men than we got on our whole force. One murder in this town makes them insecure."

"It makes me insecure."

"I guess that's funny. They want crime prevented. There is no way to prevent a crime."

"There has to be," Masuto said.

"What does that mean?"

"Those three women are going to die unless we prevent it."

"Well, you got Beckman living in there, living the life of a goddamn gigolo, with three dames waiting on him hand and foot. What else can I do? I told you you could have cops outside, front and back, but you didn't want that. We could put another cop inside, and if they start screaming about sixteen hours overtime, let them scream. They're going to holler about everything else. And for Christ's sake, don't let it drop that we got three murders pending. That's all I need."

"It's not a jail, Captain. Sooner or later, the women have to come out."

"Then, goddamnit, Masao, get the bastard!"

"I know who he is," Masuto said thoughtfully. "Getting him is another matter."

Wainwright exploded. "What! Did I hear you right—you miserable slant-eyed pain in the ass? Did I actually hear you say you know who this murderous mother is, and you had the crust to sit here and hear me get my ass roasted by the mayor and the city manager?"

"I have always defended you as a non-racist," Masuto said unhappily. "My eyes don't actually slant, so it's a kind of unhappy euphemism—"

"Goddamnit, I got excited! If you don't know me by now—"

"Anyway, I'm not sure."

"What do you mean, you're not sure? A moment ago, you were sure."

"Suppose I know who he is? That's an inner knowledge, based on what you might call a smell of things. Where is my proof? Where is my evidence, motive?"

"Who is he?"

Masuto shook his head.

"Goddamn you, Masao, you played this game with me before. I want to know who he is!" Wainwright shouted.

"I could be wrong."

"I've never known you to be wrong—not when you pull this kind of thing on me."

"Give me until tonight. If I don't bring him in tonight, I'll give you whatever I've got, and you can take it from there."

"Masao, don't play this game with me. If you know who he is, we can take him and find the gun. The gun will tie him in."

"He's crazy, but madness is not synonymous with stupidity. You're not dealing with a housebreaker or a mugger. If we take him now, we not only tip our hand, but we'll have to turn him loose. And if that happens, he won't make the one mistake that I think he'll make sooner or later."

"And how do you know he'll make it now?"

"Because no one's perfect and there are no perfect crimes. He made a whole series of errors, first with the éclairs, then with the candy, then with the kid and the chemist, killing again and again to cover his own blunders. He's frightened and he's in a hurry.

That's where he gave himself away. He was trapped in a moment in time, and he began to kill, and when I find that moment and find out why it trapped him, I've got him. Oh, he is very clever—but stupid at the same time. That's the pathological part of him."

"I wish I knew what in hell you're talking about. I still want his name."

"I can't talk you out of that?"

"Not this time, Masao. If anything happens to one of those three women, on top of what has already happened, this whole damn department is going up in smoke."

"If I give you his name," Masuto said slowly, "will you give me twenty-four hours? Twenty-four hours before you turn it over to the L.A. cops, twenty-four hours before you pick him up and begin to grill him?"

"That would really be tying my hands, Masao."

"No, sir. With all deference, that would be saving your neck. Because if you pick him up now, not only will his lawyer have him out of here in fifteen minutes, but he would slap this city with the biggest false arrest suit it ever entertained. And as you are fond of telling me, this is not downtown Pittsburgh. It's Beverly Hills."

Wainwright stared at him thoughtfully; then he nodded. "Okay. You got your twenty-four hours. Now give me the name."

Masuto took a pad, scribbled the name, and then handed the bit of paper to Wainwright.

"I'll be damned," Wainwright said.

"I could be wrong. Remember that."

"You're wrong about one thing. I'd think twice before I pulled him in or handed his name over to the

L.A. cops. I'd want to see some unshakable evidence."
He looked at the name again, then folded the slip of
paper and put it in his pocket. "Maybe we'll get
lucky this time."

Chapter 10

CATHERINE ADDISON

Masuto picked up his phone and dialed the Crombie number. Mitzie Fuller answered. "Well," she said, "if it isn't Mr. Inscrutable himself! Do you know what I feel like? I feel like I'm under house arrest in a banana republic. This is no life, Sergeant, and I don't like ladies enough to spend the rest of my life in their company. Either you spring us or I'm going to bust out."

"Give it until tonight," Masuto said.

"Now if you'll be our baby sitter, I might be able to relax and enjoy it."

"I'm afraid that's impossible right now. Please stay with it. Is Detective Beckman around?"

"He is always around. Only the bathrooms are safe from Detective Beckman's prowling presence. I'll call him."

Beckman got on the phone and said, "Masao, these gals are driving me nuts. Also, the phone doesn't stop. Every goddamn newspaper, TV station, and wire service in the world has been calling here. It's one thing for me to say no comment. But these dames—they talk to their friends. So whatever stories get out, don't blame me. I'm just the keeper. Outside in front, we got two TV cameras and crews, maybe six reporters, and a nice sprinkling of the public. Nothing like this ever happened before on Beverly Drive."

"Just keep the doors locked. What about the picture?"

"You're right. There isn't a picture of the kid anywhere in the house. I mean a framed picture, or a picture on the wall, or one of those pictures you stand on a table or a piano."

"You're sure?"

"Absolutely. But let me tell you this. In Mrs. Crombie's bedroom, I saw one of those big, classy leather-covered picture albums. I leafed through it, and, Masao, every picture in it is the daughter Kelly."

"How do you know it's Kelly?"

"Well, it's obvious, isn't it? Unless there's some other kid in Mrs. Crombie's life. Oh, it's the daughter, all right, and it starts with her as an infant and takes her right through, I guess until right before she died. If you want one of the pictures, I can slip it out. Who knows if she ever looks at the book."

"No—not yet. I think I can get a picture somewhere else. Now look, keep those women inside."

"I'll try."

Masuto was on his way out when Wainwright called after him. "Hold on a moment, Masao. One thing."

"Yes?"

"Why does he have to kill all the women?"

"Then there's no motive—or four motives."

"You mean that cold-blooded bastard would kill four women just to lay down a smoke-screen?"

"He's running scared and he has a lot to protect. He's killed three people already. A man like that is totally without conscience or morality. He will kill a human being the way you or I might kill a fly. You read about that kind of thing. There was that fellow in Texas who killed eleven people. You just don't look for it in a place like this."

"Which one of the four is he after?"

"I'm not sure. I could guess, but I'm not sure."

"Alice Greene?"

"I'm just not sure."

"And you don't think he'll drop it now?"

"He can't drop it. It has him by the throat."

"Which is what worries me, Masao. If anything happens to one of those women, we're in it up to our ears. At this point, I don't give a damn about the cost. I can put four men around that house day and night."

"No."

"Why not?"

"Because that's not the problem. The problem is keeping them in the house. I'll go down the line on the fact that nothing will happen to them while they're there. But we can't keep them there. You know by now the kind of women we deal with in Beverly Hills. They've had it their own way; they've always had it their own way. All I can do is ask them to stay there, and maybe while they're scared enough they will. But the fear will wear off, and my guess is that by tomorrow, no force on earth can keep them there. But while they're there, Beckman is with them, and there's no one I'd trust more than Beckman in a situation like that."

"All right," Wainwright agreed uneasily. "Where are you off to now?"

"Downtown—oh, I am stupid, I don't have a brain in my head." He broke off and stalked back to his office and called the Crombie house again. This time, the phone was busy. He kept dialing, looking at his watch, dialing. It was eleven o'clock. The day was running away.

Beckman answered the phone.

"Sy, did you get her first husband's name?"

"Whose first husband's name?"

"Crombie's."

"Yeah. I forgot to tell you. She was married to a guy named Neville Addison. He invented a type of radar for use on small military vehicles and made himself millions. From what I've been able to get from Mrs. Legett"—he dropped his voice—"this Crombie dame is worth millions, but millions."

"Good enough," Masuto said. "Hang in there."

Outside, the press was waiting, pleading with him. "Come on, Sergeant, open up. Give us something. Is the Mafia established in Beverly Hills?"

"Is this a contract job?"

"How does Monte Sweet fit into it?"

"Where is Monte Sweet?"

"Was he romancing this broad? Come on, give."

Masuto got into his car and drove away. He was totally into it now, putting it together, piece by piece. He felt that he had most of the pieces, the only trouble being that the most important pieces were blank. He felt driven, compelled. The shadow figure who opposed him was locked with him in combat. Masuto knew, and by now the killer was aware that Masuto knew.

He pulled his car into the parking lot at the Los Angeles Police Department and went inside. On a day when every minute counted, luck was with him. Lieutenant Pete Bones was at his desk.

Bones regarded him sourly.

"I know," Masuto said, "but if you could wrap up those two killings you got and maybe fish another one out of the bin, you wouldn't hate me so much. Right?"

"I don't hate you. You're just one curious son of a bitch, and that pisses me off. What the hell have you got, some kind of lousy Oriental crystal ball?"

"Come on now, Pete," Masuto said gently.

"How in hell did you know that those two bullets would match up?"

"Two bullets?"

"You know damn well what I'm talking about. The bullet that killed the Chicano kid and the bullet that killed the chemist."

"Same gun?" Masuto said innocently.

"You know, if it was anyone else, I'd say you're mixed up in something, but the word is you're an honest cop. Not that I'm taking my hat off to the Beverly Hills Police Department."

"No," Masuto agreed. "Of course not."

"All right. You got this thing with the botulism. Omi Saiku filled me in on that. It had to be a chemist, and you figured the chemist had to be dirty, so there was a dirty chemist somewhere whom we might have picked up, and if we put the screws on him, he would have implicated your killer. So your man killed him. You laid that out uptown. But how in hell could you be sure that the Chicano kid tied into it?"

"I don't know how many plainclothes detectives you have in the L.A. force," Masuto said. "Perhaps a thousand. We don't have enough to make up a good poker game. So I have to guess. Sometimes I guess right."

"Let me make a guess," Bones said, "that the killing you had last night ties into this."

"That's good guessing."

"Nah! Not even smart. We got a Chicano house-maid who dies of botulism who works for this Crombie woman, and then we got this Mafia-type killing in her front yard."

"Is that what you think?" Masuto asked. "The Mafia?"

"Do you?"

Masuto shook his head.

"Then what the hell are you asking me for? What am I, some kind of schmuck? When the Mafia comes into this county, I will know about it, and if they put out a contract, I'll know about that too. I'm not saying I can make an arrest stick, but I will know about it."

"Let's pretend we're on the same side," Masuto said, smiling. "I'm not trying to do you in. I come bearing gifts."

"What kind of gifts? And what do you want?"

"Only a little help."

"Yeah. What kind of gifts?"

"We have four murders," Masuto said. "Three of them took place in Los Angeles."

"That Chicano maid was working in your town."

"Yes, but she went home to L.A. before she ate those éclairs. So technically, it's yours. We don't want any more killings than we have to have. Now I think I can clear this up before midnight today, and if I do, I give you my word I'll call you in for the arrest."

"You can't do that even if you wanted to, which I don't believe for a minute."

"You know I can. I'll get through to you or to whoever you designate, and you have a car cutting through Beverly Hills, and I'll put out an assist and your car picks it up and makes the technical arrest."

"No. It's clumsy."

"If I already have the man? I'll tell you something else, when I go after him, I may very well be in Los Angeles. I can't say at this point."

"You know, Masuto, every time I see you, you got trouble for me. Every time I see you, you got some crazy project. You come here and tell me you got a killer lined up and you want to hand him over to me. Why?"

"Justice. More killings on your turf."

"Bullshit. You know who the killer is, give me his name and we'll do the rest. We're not the worst police force in the world."

"Maybe the best. We're not up to names. But you can't tell me it won't be a feather in your cap to clear up four killings."

Bones leaned back in his chair and stared at Masuto. Finally, he nodded. "Okay. We got a deal. But don't rat on me. If you do, I'll take it out of your hide. Now what do you want in exchange?"

"Very little. Perhaps a month or two more than three years ago, a young woman whose name was Catherine Addison was killed in a car crash. I want to know exactly when and where the accident took place. I want you to locate the policeman or policemen who attended the accident at the time and I want to talk to them, and if you assigned an investigator to the case, I want to talk to him as well."

Bones grinned slowly. "You got to be kidding."

"Oh, no. I'm very serious."

"Three years ago? Are you crazy, Masuto? Suppose no other car was involved in the accident? Suppose no one was booked? Suppose it didn't even happen in Los Angeles? Did it?"

"I don't know."

"You got a lot of nerve coming down here with something like this."

"I know."

He opened the pad in front of him. "What did you say her name was?"

"Catherine Addison."

"Hasn't she got relatives, a family? There are easier ways to get at this."

"She has a mother who won't talk about her. My guess is that the mother can't talk about her, and I haven't got time for psychoanalysis."

"All right, we'll give it a try."

"I want it quick."

"Yeah? I want the moon."

"Even if you find one of the cops, have him call our station. Polly there will patch him through to wherever I am."

Back in his car, Masuto felt a certain satisfaction. It was beginning to come together. Very slowly, yet it was beginning to come together.

He drove back to Beverly Hills and Beverly Drive. The media had given up, and, except for a couple of curious kids, there was no one in front of the Crombie house. Still in the driveway were three cars, the Porsche, the Seville, and Beckman's Ford. Masuto parked behind the Ford, walked to the door, and touched the bell.

There was a peephole, and he could imagine Beckman staring at him. Then the door opened.

"I'm being relieved," Beckman said. "You're taking over."

"No such luck. Where are the ladies?"

"Inside playing bridge. I'm the dummy. It don't matter that I can't play bridge worth a damn. They taught me that game and now I'm trapped, and every lousy play I make, that Crombie dame rakes me over the coals. She is a lulu. Tell you something else, Masao, with these three dames locked up together, their love for each other is going downhill swiftly. They're beginning to snap and snarl, especially the two older ones."

At that moment, Laura Crombie's voice. "Mr. Beckman, what's going on out there?"

"Sergeant Masuto. We'll be in in a moment."

"It's your deal."

"Sy," Masuto said softly, "I want one of the pictures. Kelly, Catherine. The Crombie kid. Grown, not as a child. Take it out of the album."

"We could ask. I hate to steal it."

"Mr. Beckman!" from inside.

"We are not stealing it. We're borrowing it. Don't worry. We'll put it back."

"Okay," Beckman said.

"While I'm here. I only have a few minutes."

Beckman shook his head.

"Don't worry. I'll send you upstairs," Masuto said.

Beckman led him through the house to a bright, beautifully-decorated breakfast room that overlooked the gardens and pool. The furniture was bamboo and flowered chintz, the floor was of imported Spanish tile, and the bay window set in shiny brass fittings. There were plants and flowers everywhere, and Masuto looked at it with such pleasure that Laura Crombie abandoned her tight-lipped expression of annoyance.

"You like the room, Sergeant?"

"Very much." He turned to Beckman. "Go through the house while I'm here, Sy."

"Again?" Mrs. Crombie asked.

"Please. Then I can report back that he checked the house while I was present."

Beckman strode out on his mission, and Nancy Legett said, "Sometimes, Sergeant, I wonder whether you are not a little mad. This whole notion that someone is trying to murder us—"

"Stop that, Nancy!" Laura Crombie said sharply.

Nancy Legett began to cry. She sat bent over the table on which the cards had been dealt, her body wracked with sobs. Mitzie Fuller put her arms around her.

"Come on now, darling," Mitzie said. "Everything's going to be all right."

"Nothing's going to be all right," she sobbed. "We're all going to be killed, the way Alice was killed. You know that. I know that. He killed Alice first, and then it's our turn."

"Who killed Alice?" Masuto asked gently.

"Arthur Crombie. Didn't you know?"

"No, no, that's too much," Laura Crombie said. "Now see here, Nancy, we're old friends, but that doesn't give you the right to carry on like this."

"I wish I could stay, but I can't," Masuto said firmly. "Now listen to me!"

They stopped squabbling and turned to him. Mitzie said cheerfully, "Right on, Charlie Chan. Oh, no. That was terrible of me. That was inexcusable of me. Please forgive me."

"More inexcusable since I am a Nisei, which means of Japanese parents. However, I'll forgive you."

"Bless you." She leaped up and kissed his cheek. "There's my apology."

"Thank you. Now, I want a picture of each of your ex-husbands."

"You're kidding," Laura Crombie said.

"Dead serious. Of course, Mrs. Greene presents a problem."

"You read the *Times*," Mitzie said. "You are one strange detective."

"How do you know I read the *Times*?"

"Because the *Examiner* has a picture of Alice and her ex right there on the front page. I'll tear it out for you."

"Mrs. Crombie?"

"I'll find a picture of Arthur for you."

"Mrs. Legett?"

She was unwilling to meet his gaze.

"Mrs. Legett, did you hear me? I have to have a picture of your ex-husband."

Still avoiding his gaze, blushing, she opened her purse and took a two-by-three photo out of her billfold. She handed it to Masuto. The two other women stared at her in disbelief, and then, unable to contain herself, Mitzie cried out, "Oh, no! I don't believe it."

"That's enough," Laura Crombie snapped.

"And you, Mrs. Fuller?" Masuto asked Mitzie.

"I've insulted you and kissed you, so no more of that Mrs. Fuller stuff. Mitzie. I've decided you remind me of Richard Boone, only you're better looking. As for a picture, I wouldn't have that little bastard's picture within a mile of me. But all you have to do is call the studio."

"Metro?"

"That's right. That's where sonnyboy is shooting his new picture."

"I'll be there in an hour."

"You will? I knew it! I knew it! I knew that little son of a bitch is the one. Oh, I hope you get him, Masuto. And I hope they have public seating at the gas chamber. I want to be there, right in front."

"Mitzie, how can you!" Nancy cried.

"It's easy."

"I'll get the picture for you," Laura Crombie said.

On the way out of the house, Beckman slid the picture of Catherine Addison into Masuto's side pocket.

"There's a possibility that Polly will put a call in to here," Masuto said to Beckman, "from an L.A. cop. I'm going to stop off at my house and then I'm going on to Metro. So you'll catch up with me in either place."

Chapter 11

THE DIRECTOR
AND THE PRODUCER

Long ago, it was said that no one knows Brooklyn, the suggestion implicit being that even if one set out to master such knowledge, the quest would be fruitless. The same might be said of Los Angeles. Long, long ago, the vast California county of Los Angeles contained dozens and dozens of separate towns and villages and cities, Los Angeles City being the largest. Through the years, under the impetus of urban sprawl and enormous population growth, these dozens of cities had come together, the way cookie dough placed too close on the cookie sheet will spread and join. Masuto worked in Beverly Hills, which was almost entirely surrounded by metropolitan Los Angeles; he lived in Culver City, which was another enclave into Los Angeles, and the studios of Metro-Goldwyn-Mayer were also in Culver City.

But there was no non-urban countryside to be crossed between Culver City and Beverly Hills, or between the two of them and Los Angeles. The streets of one merged into the streets of the other, and even the oldest citizens would have been hard pressed to tell you what constituted the border between one place and another.

Usually, driving from work to his home, Masuto would take Motor Avenue or Overland Avenue south from the Twentieth Century-Fox Studios on Pico Boulevard. Both routes were in the direction of the MGM Studios, which were less than a mile from Masuto's home. Perhaps Motor Avenue passed closer to his house. Masuto drove that way, and a few minutes before one, he parked in the driveway of his house.

Kati, who was vacuuming the living room, let out a squeal of surprise as he entered. "Masao, what is it? What happened?"

"Nothing happened."

"You're afraid to tell me. I don't care. I'm just so happy to see you. I don't care."

"What don't you care about?"

"You've been fired. All right. Good. I never enjoyed having a policeman for a husband."

"I haven't been fired. I'm going to MGM, and this is on the way, and I'm tired of eating junk food. I thought that if I stopped off here, I'd get a decent lunch. But maybe with the consciousness-raising, you haven't got the time or inclination, and if that's the case I'll understand."

"Stop teasing me. I have tempura all prepared for tonight, but you may just call me and tell me that you're having dinner with four more women—"

"I might."

"I have shrimp and string beans and sweet potato and zucchini all cleaned and ready."

"It sounds incredible."

He sat at the kitchen table, while the room filled with the delicious smell of deep fried shrimp and vegetables. He had the pictures spread out in front of him, the three men and the girl.

"What do you think of Monte Sweet?" he asked Kati.

"Monte Sweet?"

"The comic. You've seen him on television."

"The one who hates everyone. Oh, no, I can't bear to watch him, he's so filled with hatred and rage. How can a man be so terrible?"

"It's his stock in trade."

"Why is it funny to say terrible things about other people?"

"Perhaps all humor consists of a kind of hatred. We laugh at the suffering of others."

"I don't."

"Because you, Kati, are a very special person."

She placed the platter of tempura and a bowl of rice in front of him, and Masuto picked up his ivory chopsticks, reflecting on what a pleasure it was to eat with these beautiful artifacts rather than with the barbaric knife and fork, which turned an approach to food into an attack.

"What are those pictures?" Kati asked him.

"The men were once married to the women whose lives are threatened."

"And the lovely girl?"

"Tell me, Kati. What do you see in her face?"

"Very open, very trusting."

"Yes, I think so. Your tempura, as always, is brilliant."

"How can tempura be brilliant?"

"Ah, believe me. Why don't you sit down and eat with me?"

"Because I ate an hour ago," Kati said. "Now that my consciousness has been raised at least a little bit, I can enjoy the position of the Japanese housewife who serves her husband hand and foot. I don't mean that I really enjoy it, but I can see what I am doing objectively and I know something about what a male chauvinist pig actually is."

"You mean all that in one session?"

"I don't think you are a male chauvinist pig, Masao. That's a terrible thing to say. It makes me uncomfortable."

"And you're not a Japanese housewife."

"You mean they don't have vacuum cleaners?"

"No. I understand Japan is quite advanced. But you happen to be a very beautiful American woman."

"Ah so! Really!"

She was blushing, Masuto realized, and as he finished eating and stood up and kissed her, the telephone rang.

"Not in the middle of the day," Kati said. She pulled away from him and picked up the phone. "For you, Masao."

"Yes, this is Masuto," he said.

"This is Officer Commager, L.A.P.D. Lieutenant Bones said you wanted to talk to me."

"About the Catherine Addison case?" Masuto asked.

"That's right."

"Good! Great! How did he find you so quickly?"

"He put the word into the Hollywood and North Hollywood Stations. I guess he found out that it happened on Mulholland Drive."

"Did you say Mulholland Drive?"

"Yes, sir."

"Well, I'll be damned. Do you have the exact date?" He covered the phone. "Kati—pen and paper."

She brought him a pad and a pen.

"Yes, sir. It was March third, nineteen seventy-five."

"Time?"

"We estimated that she went over the cliffside at

about eight o'clock. It would be dark at that time of year."

"You've got a good memory, Commager."

"No, sir. The truth is that I barely recalled the case at first. But Lieutenant Bones had them pull my report from the files. I have it right here in front of me."

"Good, good. Now exactly where did this happen?"

"You know, Sergeant, we got to draw maps for this kind of thing. On Mulholland, for anything between Laurel Canyon and Coldwater Canyon, we take our measurements from the crossroads. In this case, from the point where Laurel Canyon Boulevard crosses Mulholland Drive. Measuring west from there—you really want this exactly? You know, it was three years ago."

"As precisely as you can give it to me."

"Okay, Sergeant. Measuring west from the Laurel Canyon crossover, you drive exactly one mile and seven twentieths. There the road curves to the left. On the left you have the high shoulder of the hill, on the right a sheer drop of about a hundred feet."

"I think I know the spot. But I don't remember a perpendicular drop."

"I don't mean absolutely perpendicular, Sergeant. There is a slight slope that's covered with chaparral, but it might just as well be perpendicular for anything that goes over there. Now this Addison kid's car was coming from the east, from Laurel Canyon, and she must have lost control, because instead of making the curve she went straight ahead and over."

"At what speed?"

"You know that's only an estimate," Commager said. "But we get pretty good at that kind of thing. I got down here in my notes that she was moving at thirty miles an hour."

"Were there brake marks where she went over?"

"No."

"How did you account for that? Was her brakeline cut or broken? Was her brake fluid gone?"

"No, sir."

"Are you telling me that there were no skid marks and you didn't come up with an explanation? Or a question?"

"Now hold on, Sergeant. We're not halfwits. We knew she didn't try to break her speed. If she had, then the car would have tumbled over the edge of the road and there would have been broken brush from there on down. But there wasn't any broken brush under the road. She went over the side like the car was shot out of a catapult. That's the way we figured the thirty miles an hour. It maybe don't sound like much speed on a highway, but over the side of a cliff, it's a hell of a lot of speed."

"It could have been fifteen or twenty miles an hour?"

"I suppose so."

"A man who knows a little mechanics can wire a throttle down. Then he throws the car into gear and jumps out. Did you look for that kind of a device?"

"We had no reason to. It went down as an accidental death."

"What did the autopsy show?"

"My God, Sergeant, that car tumbled down maybe over a hundred feet and then burst into flames. There wasn't much left of the car or the kid inside of it."

"How was she identified?"

"Her purse was thrown clear. Then her rings, dental work, the usual thing."

"Did her mother make an identification?"

"I can't tell you that, Sergeant. That would happen downtown. But in the normal course of events they would call her in for an I.D."

"Were there any witnesses?"

"Not to the crash. People saw the flames and called us."

"What kind of a car was it?"

"A little red car. It must have been a beauty, one of those little convertible Mercedes."

"Red?"

"That's right, red."

For a long moment of silence, Masuto sat with the telephone in his hand.

"You still there, Sergeant?"

"One more point, Officer Commager. You've been very helpful, and now I'm going to ask you to do the impossible. Close your eyes and go back to that night. You're in a radio car, a black-and-white. You get the call. Where are you when that call comes in?"

"Southbound on Laurel, going up the hill."

"All right—up the hill, and you turn right onto Mulholland. Now between that point and the place where the car is, did you see a man on foot?"

Now the silence was on Officer Commager's end. Kati watched Masuto's tense face as he listened and waited. She did not often see him at moments like this, and she was not sure she liked him like this, his nostrils quivering slightly, his ordinarily placid brown face suddenly the face of the hunter.

"Jesus Christ," Commager burst out, "this is crazy. I see these characters on the witness stand giving testimony from five, six years ago—this is only three years ago and it's like a dream. I think I saw a man on foot, and then I don't know. If you put me on the witness stand, a lawyer could tear it to shreds. I think so, but I can't swear to it. It was nighttime, and I was responding to a call."

"You've done nobly," Masuto said. "Thank you. Maybe this will save some lives."

He put down the phone and sat and stared at the notes he had made.

"Masao?" Kati said.

"Yes?"

"Whose lives will be saved?"

"Three woman—if I am lucky, if something breaks in this lunatic puzzle. I keep moving, but he moves faster."

"Will you be careful?"

He kissed her again and went out to his car.

During the short ride from his house to the sprawling Metro-Goldwyn-Mayer lot, Masuto speculated on whether he should have called the studio and made an appointment with Billy Fuller, the director. Then he shrugged it off. He had no time for second thoughts. He'd manage.

The guard at the gate said, "Mister, if you don't have a pass, if nobody put your name on my list, I don't let you in."

"I'm Detective Sergeant Masuto of the Beverly Hills Police." He showed his badge.

"That cuts no ice here. This is Culver City."

"What would cut ice? Suppose I took you in for obstructing justice?"

"Here? In Culver City?"

"Now look, this is a homicide investigation. If you don't think I can arrest you right here in Culver City, I suggest you pick up your phone and call the local cops. Meanwhile, I'll be talking to whoever runs this place. Or we can settle it cool and civilized. Which is it?"

"Okay. You win. Billy Fuller?"

"That's right."

"He's shooting on Stage Three. That's the trouble, Sergeant. I can get my ass burned right off if he wants to be nasty."

"Lay it on me."

Masuto parked his car. Then he walked through the gate and found Stage Three. A red light was swinging lazily outside the door of the sound stage, an indication that inside filming was in progress. Masuto knew enough about film studios to know that no take, as they called it, lasted more than a few minutes at most; and when the red light went out, he entered the dark, cavernous interior. Coming out of the brilliant sunshine, the comparative darkness was impenetrable at first, and he stood for a minute or two, waiting for his eyes to adjust. Bit by bit, he made out the jungle of wires and cables that confronted him. The scene was being shot at the other end of the sound stage, the view blocked by a set of flats. Masuto walked carefully toward it, and then, coming around in a circle, he was confronted by a brightly-lit New York summer street scene, a Greenwich Village café, tables, actors, cameramen, grips, electricians—and a man who barred his way and told him that this was a closed set.

"I'm looking for William Fuller."

"He's on the set, mister. We're shooting, and he can't be disturbed. And like I said, this set is closed. So I suggest you call his office and make an appointment."

"I have to see him now," Masuto said.

"Buzz off, yes? Don't give us a hard time. Or do I have to call the studio cops?"

"I'm Sergeant Masuto, Beverly Hills police. I suggest you let me talk to Mr. Fuller."

By now, a circle of people had gathered around. A small man, about five feet seven inches in height, energetic, tight, with long hair and a lean, birdlike face, dressed in blue jeans and a blue work shirt, pushed into the circle and demanded, "What in hell goes on here? I'm trying to make a movie."

"This clown says he's a cop and he wants to talk to you."

"This clown," Masuto said coldly, "is used to being addressed as Detective Sergeant Masuto." He took out his badge. "Now here's my badge. I'm investigating a homicide. If you're William Fuller, I'd like ten minutes of your time, in a place where we can talk privately."

Evidently, it was Fuller. "Are you nuts?" he demanded. "We're in the middle of shooting. Do you know what it's going to cost if we close shop now?"

"I'm not asking you to close shop. I'm asking for ten minutes of your time."

"It's impossible. Forget it. I don't know one goddamn thing about any homicide, so forget it."

"All right." Masuto nodded. "I get a warrant and I pull you in as a material witness. We hold you twenty-four hours. What will that cost?"

"You wouldn't dare. Jesus, I live in Beverly Hills. I pull some weight there. God damn it, you're going to hear about this."

"Well, which is it? The easy way or the hard way?"

Billy Fuller stared at Masuto. Then he turned to the circle of people and snapped, "Take ten! But stay close!" Then he motioned to Masuto and led him past the set to a line of portable dressing rooms. "In here." It was fitted out as a small office, with a desk and several chairs.

"Now what the hell is this all about?" Fuller wanted to know. He dropped into a chair. Masuto sat facing him.

"Last night a woman named Alice Greene was killed."

"You mean that thing on Beverly Drive?"

"Yes."

"I don't know the dame from Adam. Never met her."

"She was a friend of your ex-wife, Mitzie."

"I don't know her either. The bitch doesn't exist."

"She exists," Masuto assured him quietly. "I want her to continue to exist. She's in very great danger. The same man who killed Alice Greene is trying to kill her."

"Come on!"

"Believe me."

"Look, you came to the wrong party. I don't start any defense fund. If someone is looking to finish off Mitzie, he doesn't get my help. But I don't interfere either."

"I see. Are you by any chance planning to kill her?" Masuto asked quietly.

"What are you, crazy? I'm in the middle of a picture, and you're asking me am I planning to kill some miserable broad." He shook his head. "Are we finished? I told you I don't know this Greene woman. You want to know would I kill Mitzie? Maybe. If I could get away with it. If I could find enough time between pictures."

"That's a lot of hate. Why?"

"That, Mr. Detective, is none of your goddamn business."

"Why did your marriage break up?"

"What are you, the Louella Parsons of the Beverly Hills cops?"

"It's very important that you answer that question."

"Not to me." He got to his feet.

"A few more questions, Mr. Fuller. Were you in the service?"

"Yes, I spent a lousy year in Nam with an army film unit. But you know what occurs to me? I don't have to answer any one of your damn questions. You blackmailed me out there, telling me you'd kill a day's shooting if I didn't talk to you. I think I'll talk to my lawyer about that."

"You could do that," Masuto agreed. "But I think it would be easier to spend a few minutes more with me and not lose the day's shooting. You can still take it up with your lawyer."

"Okay, okay, let's get it over with."

"Do you own a pistol?"

"Four of them, and I got the papers on all of them."

"What kind?"

"I have a Colt forty-five hogleg." For the first time, his tight face relaxed slightly and he smiled thinly. "That's a reproduction of the old frontier Colt, bring down a man at a hundred yards, blow a hole through you big as a saucer. I got a Browning thirty-caliber automatic and I own two target pistols, both of them twenty-two."

"What kind of guns are the twenty-twos?"

He was relaxed now. He enjoyed talking about guns. "One is an old Smith and Wesson hand ejector.

It's got to be fifty years old, but perfect. A little pocket gun, but a beauty. That's the one I carry when I carry a gun."

"You carry a gun?"

"Not now. At night."

"Why?"

"Man, you got to be kidding. Do you read the newspapers?"

"Sometimes. And the other twenty-two?"

"That's a Browning target pistol. Automatic, and it fires twenty-two longs."

"Where do you keep your guns?"

"Like I said, sometimes I carry the little piece at night. I keep the thirty-caliber in my desk, and the hogleg and the target gun have the usual plush-lined boxes. I keep both boxes in my study."

"Where do you live, Mr. Fuller?"

"I don't see where the hell all this fits in."

"If you will bear with me just a few minutes more," Masuto said softly, "we can finish this and you can go back to your work. I was asking where you live."

"I rent a little house on Camden. I had a goddamn mansion on Palm Drive, but it went to that bitch. You know, this is the age of the ripoff and the land of the ripoff. But there's one ripoff that cuts everything else down to size. Divorce. I pay that bitch four thousand clams a month. I had to give her the house. We're talking about that target pistol. She gave me that. The one goddamn thing she ever gave me, except maybe a dose of the clap. Nah! I'm only talking. The only dose she gave me was a dose of herself, and that was plenty."

"She gave you the target pistol?"

"So she did."

"You said it came in a large, wooden box?"

"Right."

"Who takes care of your house?"

"I got a housekeeper, a black lady. She comes in every morning, leaves at nine."

"Then she's there now?"

"Certainly."

"When," Masuto asked him, "did you last look at the target pistol?"

"When? Jesus, I don't know. This film you're lousing up right now—I been with it three weeks. I know I haven't touched the pistol in that time."

"I suggest to you that it's not there."

"What's not there?"

"The target pistol."

"You got to be kidding. What are you trying to tell me?"

"I'm saying it was stolen."

"What! How the hell would you know? You mean one of your guys picked up a target pistol? Who says it's mine?"

Masuto shrugged.

Fuller picked up the telephone on his desk and dialed a number. Masuto could hear, faintly, the voice of the woman who answered. Fuller said, "Lanie, this is Mr. Fuller. I want you to go into my study and open the rosewood box on my desk and tell me what's in it. You know, there are two boxes. There's a black teak box that I keep locked. Look in the other box, the reddish one." There was a pause. "Yes, I'll hold the wire."

He stood there with the telephone in his hand, watching Masuto. It had become a game, and it had caught his attention. "You know," he said to Masuto, "they keep arguing, does art imitate life or does life imitate art—I mean if you can call movies art. I mean this kind of a ploy is exactly what one of those movie detectives would pull. Then, if the gun's still there, all you got to say to me is, Sue me. So I'm wrong."

The phone demanded his attention again. He listened. Then he said, "Thanks, Lanie. No, it's okay." He put down the telephone and stared at Masuto.

"The gun is gone," Masuto said.

"How the devil did you know?"

Masuto shrugged.

"Stolen?"

"You didn't give it to anyone?"

"What does that mean?"

Again, Masuto shrugged.

"So the gun is gone. What do I do now?"

"I suggest you call the Beverly Hills Police and report it. Give them the serial number and the registration number."

"I'm reporting it to you."

"That won't do. By the way, where were you last night, between ten and eleven o'clock?"

"Come on, what in hell is this?"

"I told you. It's a homicide investigation."

"All right. I was home."

"Alone?"

"Alone, in bed, reading a screenplay. After a day in this place, I don't even want to get laid."

"No witnesses, no one to vouch that you were there?"

"Just tell me one thing, mister—what are you trying to accuse me of? Of murdering this Alice Greene, who I never even laid eyes on? Or of planning to murder Mitzie? If it's a crime to plan a murder, you can take me in right now. Oh, shit, the hell with it! I got a film to make."

Masuto stood up. "All right, Mr. Fuller. Don't forget to call in about the gun. By the way"—he held out the snapshot of Catherine Addison—"do you know this girl?"

He glanced at the picture without interest. "Should I?"

"I don't know. Would you take a good look at it?"

Fuller stared at the picture for a moment. "Good-looking kid, but the woods are full of them. No, I don't know her."

Masuto nodded and put the picture back in his pocket. As he left the soundstage, the strident voice of Billy Fuller was calling the actors back to their places. Outside, the blazing sunlight blinded Masuto as much as the darkness had previously, and squinting, he walked back to the guard at the gate.

"How'd it come out?" the guard asked him.

"Not too bad. Tell me, isn't Fulton Legett here on this lot?"

"Going down the list, huh?" The guard nodded and pointed. "Over there in the executive building."

"Are you going to give me a hard time again?"

"You're really a Beverly Hills cop?"

For the second time, Masuto took out his badge and exhibited it.

"I didn't know they had plainclothes cops on the Beverly Hills force."

"They even have them in uniform," Masuto said. "I'll step in there and have a word with Mr. Legett."

Inside, there was another guard at the desk, and once again Masuto went through the routine.

"I'll call up," the guard said.

"Why don't you let me surprise him?"

"What is this? Are you going to make some kind of arrest?"

"No arrest. But I have some questions for him. If you call up there, and he says he won't see me, and then I go up there anyway, you're in hot water. This way, you just figured it was okay for me to go up. You can't get into trouble."

"He's in room six eleven."

"Thanks."

The girl in six eleven—Masuto decided she was receptionist and secretary—looked up at him in surprise and said that they were not casting. She was a very pretty girl, with blonde hair and wide blue eyes.

"I'm not here for casting. I wish to see Mr. Legett."

"Oh? Did you have an appointment, mister—?"

"Detective Sergeant Masuto. Beverly Hills police."

"Oh? Are you sure it's Mr. Fulton Legett you wish to see?"

"Quite sure."

"And you're sure you're a policeman? I never saw a Chinese policeman before."

"I'm a policeman," Masuto said, showing her his badge.

She pressed a button on her telephone and said unhappily, "F.L., there's a policeman here to see you." She listened for a moment and then said plaintively, "He asked me if I'm sure you're a policeman and not one of the studio guards. He thinks I can't tell the difference between a policeman and a studio guard. That's hitting below the belt, isn't it?"

"Absolutely."

"Through that door," she said, pointing.

Masuto opened the door and went into a large, square carpeted and wood-paneled room. The furnishings were all chrome and leather, with glass-topped tables and non-objective paintings on the walls. Fulton Legett sat behind a very large desk. He was a short, overweight man who looked more than his fifty years. He had pudgy hands with well-manicured nails, nails polished to a high sheen, and he had a small cupid's bow of a mouth.

"Are you sure you want to see me?" Legett asked.

Masuto nodded. "Sergeant Masuto, Beverly Hills police." He held out his badge.

"Ah, I see. I suppose it's about that terrible thing at the Crombie house. Poor Alice. She deserved better."

"Then you knew Mrs. Greene?"

"Oh, indeed, indeed. Knew her very well. I called Laura as soon as I saw it in the papers."

"You knew Mrs. Crombie?"

"Oh, yes. Yes, indeed."

"Do you know Mitzie Fuller?"

Legett's eyes narrowed. He hesitated a moment too long. "No," he said shortly.

"But you do know Billy Fuller?"

"Of course I know the little son of a bitch. We're on the same lot. He's got a head as big as the Goodyear balloon. I've showed him a few scripts, nothing good enough for the little king—" He had forgotten grief and the dead; he was a producer whose scripts had been turned down by a director.

Masuto interrupted. "Your ex-wife, Nancy—"

"Yes, I spoke to her."

"When?"

"When I called Laura Crombie. Nancy told me about the situation there. I just can't believe it—that there's some bloodthirsty lunatic out to kill those women."

"There is."

"Well, damn it, it's one of those things that are hard to believe. Who would want to kill Nancy?"

"I don't know." Masuto shrugged. "Would you?"

"Are you serious?"

"I only meant would you know anyone who might want to kill her. I didn't mean to suggest that you might want to kill her. But since you appear to take it that way, I'll ask you. Would you want to kill her?"

"That's a hell of a question."

"Yes, I suppose so. But Mrs. Legett suggested it."

"What? You mean she said I wanted to kill her?"

"Not exactly. But when I asked her who might want her dead, she pointed to you."

"That miserable, crazy woman!"

"Oh? Then I take it she was responding emotionally."

"What a lousy thing to say! I give that woman blood. Practically every nickel I got goes to paying my alimony. She is loaded. Loaded. That house of mine—which is now hers—up on Lexington Road is one of the best pieces of property in Beverly Hills. It would fetch a million, and from an Arab or an Iranian, maybe a million and a half, and she's got it and I eat at Hamburg Hamlet. And now she tells the cops that I'm out to murder her. You know something," he snapped at Masuto, "it's not a bad idea. If I knew where to buy one of those contracts you see in films, I wouldn't mind putting it out on her."

"That's not anything to tell me."

"The hell with it! Who gives a damn?"

"Do you own a gun?" Masuto asked him.

"A gun? What in hell would I do with a gun?"

"Then you don't own one?"

"No, of course not."

"I asked you about Mitzie Fuller before," Masuto said.

"Yeah?"

"You said you don't know her."

"You're sitting here," Legett said, "because you bulled your way into my office and I let it be. I don't have to answer one goddamn question. As a matter of fact, I can have you thrown out of here. You're a small town cop who's off his range."

"You called Mitzie Fuller a number of times, asking for a date. Why deny it? You're divorced."

"You have got one stinking nerve."

Masuto slid Catherine Addison's picture across the desk. Legett glanced down at it. "What's this? That's Kelly. What has she got to do with all of this?"

"You knew her?"

"Of course I knew her. She was Laura's kid." He pushed the picture back at Masuto. "That's enough. Get out."

Masuto put the picture in his pocket and left.

Chapter 12

MONTE SWEET

Masuto was building his structure, but it was still a house of cards, fragile, unsupported. He had written the name of the murderer down on a slip of paper and had handed it to Wainwright, but that was a gesture, a touch of ego that he was almost ashamed of, and always there was the possibility that he could be wrong. If he was wrong, then he had slandered an innocent person, and the fact that only he and Wainwright knew about the slander did not lessen his guilt. Whatever else he was—a policemen, a father, a husband, a rose-grower, a Nisei—he was still above all a Zen Buddhist with an ultimate responsibility to himself.

Yet as he picked up piece after piece, the pattern he looked for was beginning to emerge. Still, it was without meaning; he had built an arch out of intuition, psychological guesswork, and shreds of disconnected evidence. The keystone was missing.

Lost wholly in his thoughts, he ran a red light, narrowly missing a cursing motorist, and then he saw the blinking light of a Beverly Hills black-and-white behind him. He pulled over to the curb, the black-and-white behind him. The officer got out of his car, walked over and said, "Traffic lights don't mean anything to you, do they, mister?"

Then the cop bent down and said, "I'll be damned!"

"I will if I keep this up," Masuto said.

"Are you chasing something, Sergeant?" the officer asked.

"No, Macneil. The only thing I'm chasing is an idea. I just ran the light. I haven't done it in years."

Macneil shrugged. "We can't all be perfect."

"You ought to give me a ticket. I deserve it."

"Ah, the hell with it! Only keep your eyes open, Sarge. You missed that guy by inches."

Masuto drove on. He turned off Santa Monica Boulevard into the parking space behind the real estate offices of Crombie & Hawkes. Their three-story building oozed prosperity. Over the door, heavy brass letters spelled out the names of the dead Hawkes and the living Crombie. Inside, the first floor was reminiscent of a bank, with two rows of desks, four on each side, and behind each desk an attractive woman. These, Masuto surmised, were the residential agents. A broad staircase led up to the second floor, and brass letters indicated that business properties were dealt with up there. Next to the entrance a pretty blonde woman—there was a pretty blonde woman at almost every reception desk in West Los Angeles and Beverly Hills—supplied information. But then the pretty girls from every town in America poured into Los Angeles to become film stars, an ambition which very few of them ever achieved.

The pretty girl at the reception desk informed Masuto that Mr. Arthur Crombie was not in.

"When do you expect him?"

"He left for lunch. It's after three now, and he's usually back by two-thirty. So he may have had an appointment with a customer. He'll call in sooner or later."

Masuto gave her his card. "I would appreciate hearing from him when he returns."

"I'll tell him."

Back at headquarters, Wainwright intercepted Masuto. "Well, what about it, Masao? Where are we?"

"God knows."

"That's a hell of an answer. Pete Bones called. He wants to talk to you."

Dropping down behind his desk, Masuto dialed the number and asked for Bones.

The thick, throaty voice said, "Masuto?"

"Wainwright said you wanted to talk to me."

"Right. We're going to put away the chemist. No one's claimed the body, so he goes into Potter's Field. Do you want to look at the corpse before we bury it?"

It was as cold and sad and terrible as so much of the human comedy or tragedy, depending on one's point of view. A man is trained as a chemist. What did he dream of as a kid, Masuto wondered? What wonderful adventures marked his first days with test tubes and retorts? And then what began to corrode and rot, until his knowledge produced a botulin that destroyed a poor Chicano girl who never knew of his existence or of the existence of the man who hired him. And now as alone as any corpse could be, he went into the earth, unmourned, unknown, and unwanted.

"What was his name?" Masuto asked, out of a curiosity he could not repress.

"Alfred Bindler."

"Poor devil."

"The son of a bitch is not worth your sympathy.

Tell me, do you want to look or do we dump him?"

"No, I don't want to see him. Wait a moment. He was shot behind the ear?"

"Right."

"Were there powder burns?"

"No. The way we see it, the range was the whole length of the room. The killer opened the door. Bindler had his back to him. The killer raised his gun and popped him."

"Twelve feet?"

"Just about."

"If he picked his spot and Bindler was in the act of turning, that was damn good shooting."

"You can say that again."

Masuto put down the phone. Someone knocked at the door to his office.

"Come in."

He knew the face. A smallish man, balding, with protruding blue eyes and a wide mouth. It was a face millions of people knew.

"You're Sergeant Masuto?"

Masuto nodded.

"I'm Monte Sweet. They told me to see you. They told me you were in charge of the case."

"Sit down, Mr. Sweet," Masuto said.

"Yeah." He sat down in the chair next to Masuto's desk. "Yeah—look at me. I'm ugly as sin. I make a living out of that, out of being ugly and nasty and rotten. They pay me thirty grand a week to insult the yokels in Vegas. An Italian sits down in the front row, I call him a wop. My real name's Seteloni. I see you sitting there, I say, Hey, Chink, where's the laundry? Stupid stuff, and they laugh themselves sick. It turns my stomach to watch those muttonheads laughing, but that's what I do for a living and it stinks. I'm fifty-three years old. You think a guy of fifty-three can't fall in love? You think Monte Sweet couldn't love anything? Well, let me tell you different. I loved that woman the way I never loved anyone. And she loved me. God damn it to hell, she loved me! It was real! And now that lousy creep killed her."

He was shaking with emotion, tears welling out of the corners of his eyes, his hands trembling. "I'll get you some water," Masuto said.

"I could use a drink."

"I'll try."

Masuto went out of the room, closing the door behind him. Three uniformed cops were standing there. "Is that Monte Sweet you got inside?" one of them asked.

"It is."

He went into Wainwright's office. "This is a police station," Wainwright said.

"Come on, I know you keep a bottle in your desk."

"For emergencies."

"This is an emergency."

Wainwright poured into a paper cup. "What the devil goes on in there?"

"He's taking Alice Greene's death very hard. Apparently, he loved her deeply."

"You got a soft streak that laps up bullshit, Masao. Men like Monte Sweet don't love anyone deeply."

"All men love something."

"Yeah? You tell me who Monte Sweet is going to love when he discovers that his light of love left her fortune to a passel of dogs."

"Maybe he knew that. He tells me that they pay him thirty thousand dollars a week in Las Vegas. If that's the case, he can live without her fortune."

"Thirty grand a week? You believe that?"

"I read such things. He's very big there and on TV. And Alice Greene was not that rich."

"What's he here for?"

"He's mad."

"Then he ought to tell you something."

Masuto went back to his office, holding a paper cup which he gave to Sweet. "This is vodka. A police station is not a good place to look for a drink."

"Okay, okay." He took it in a single gulp, grimacing.

"Who killed Mrs. Greene?" Masuto asked him.

"Don't you know? What the hell are you—Keystone cops?"

"We have a case and we're trying to solve it."

"Oh, that's beautiful. You got a case. A woman is dead, a woman who was the best thing that ever happened to me, and you tell me that you got a case."

"You were talking about it before," Masuto said evenly. "You indicated that you knew. Who do you think killed her?"

"I don't think. I know."

"Who?"

"Alan Greene." And when there was no reaction from Masuto, he went on, "I know what you cookies think. You think because her car was wired, it was a Mafia job, and they been telling you that I'm hooked up with the Mafia. That is a carload of crap. I got no more connection with the Mafia than you have, mister, and maybe less. And who says you got to be a contract man to wire a car? I could wire a car if I had to and so could Greene. Did he tell you that he once ran a garage? No, sir. You bet your sweet patooties he didn't."

"So you think Alan Greene murdered his ex-wife. Why?"

"Because he hated her guts. He played the big macho game with her and beat her to within an inch of her life. You didn't know that?"

"No, I didn't," Masuto admitted. "You're talking about a physical beating?"

"What other kind is there?"

"How bad? Was she hospitalized?"

"You're damn right she was," Sweet said.

"What hospital?"

"They took her to Cedars-Sinai and she was there three days. After that, he didn't have a leg to stand on. She agreed to keep it quiet, and he agreed to the divorce and the settlement. He was paying her five thousand a month and he gave her the house on Roxbury Drive. I would have married her in a minute, but Alice and I agreed that we'd never let that bastard off the hook as long as he lived. Well, he got off the hook."

"Apparently he was rich enough to afford the alimony. Why should he kill her?"

"No one is rich enough to afford sixty grand a year."

"Do you inherit from Mrs. Greene?" Masuto asked him.

"Come on, if you haven't spoken to her lawyers you're lousier cops than I imagine. Her money goes to dogs. You know that. I never wanted a nickel of her money, and I'm as crazy about dogs as she was."

"Yes, of course. I was not trying to trap you. I just wondered whether you knew what was in her will."

"All right. That's your job. Now what are you going to do about Greene?"

"You make an accusation. That's not evidence."

"You bring him in and put the screws on him, and you'll get plenty of evidence."

"We don't do things that way," Masuto said.

"I just bet you don't, with your two-bit police force. If it was the L.A. cops—"

"They don't go in for torture either. But I can tell you this, Mr. Sweet. We'll have the evidence and the killer."

"When?"

"Ah, that's not easy to say."

When Monte Sweet had departed, Wainwright said to Masuto, "Well, what did he give you?"

"He said Greene once owned a garage and that he could wire a car. As a matter of fact, Sweet said he could wire a car himself."

"So where are we, Masao?"

"Closer."

"And now?"

"I think I'll try Laura Crombie again."

Chapter 13

THE BAR

Going to the Crombie house, on Beverly Drive, Masuto's car was almost sideswiped by a tourist bus. It was the second time in a single day that he had narrowly avoided an accident. It was unlike him. He had allowed himself to become submerged completely in a game of chess with an invisible antagonist—and to become absorbed in this manner was dangerous, dangerous for himself and dangerous for the women he was committed to protect.

He was crowding too much into a single day, and he was being drawn too thin, yet he could not stop. He found himself quietly cursing the tourist bus, and the fact that he could be thus irritated disturbed him. Yet, he reflected, it was ridiculous to allow these huge tourist buses to prowl the streets of Beverly Hills, adding their noxious blasts to the prevailing pollution. People from all over the country and all over the world came here to look at streets not too different from streets in any other wealthy community, content to pay their money to have the homes of movie stars pointed out to them. Masuto knew it was a swindle. Three quarters of the places pointed to as the tourists rode by in their big buses had been vacated by the stars years ago, sold and resold since then, but still giving the tour guides a reason to sell their tickets—and of course Beverly Drive, the broad main street of the town with its magnificent mansions, was the focus of all the tour buses.

Driving more carefully, he pulled into the Crombie driveway, parking behind Beckman's Ford. Beckman let him into the house.

"Quiet, very quiet, Masao," Beckman said. "The ladies are driving me crazy. I don't know if I can hold them tonight. And to make it worse, someone at the station gave my wife this number. She called here three times. Now I stopped answering the phone. I let the ladies do that."

They were standing alone in the entrance foyer, and Masuto said to Beckman, speaking softly, "Tell me about Mitzie."

"What's to tell? I'm forty-three years old, Masao. If I was fifteen years younger, I'd leave my wife and marry Mitzie. Except why the hell should she look twice at a cop who makes fifteen thousand a year? I'd have to put away three years of wages to buy that Porsche of hers."

"You've spent twenty-four hours with those women, and that's all you've got?"

"What do you want?"

"Who is she?"

"You mean where does she come from? I'm not totally a jerk, Masao. She comes from Dallas, Texas. Her mother was a laundress. Her father was a no-good bum and a drunk. Mitzie cut out of there first chance she got and came here like all the other kids do to become a movie star. She worked around as a waitress and for a while she worked in a hairdressing place."

"Wait a minute—not Tony Cooper's place?"

"That's right. She gets a big bang out of the fact

that she can go there now and lay down thirty bucks for the same service she used to dish out."

"It's a small world. Did you ever ask her why she and Billy Fuller split up?"

"There's a general consensus among all three dames that he's a son of a bitch."

"Okay, Sy. Now I want to talk to Mrs. Crombie. I'll wait here. Where are they?"

"Watching TV."

"Get her."

Laura Crombie came into the foyer with Beckman and said, "I'm sure you've solved everything, Sergeant, and we can stop living this nightmare."

"Not quite."

"Of course it can't go on, you know that. We can't continue to live here shut up and away from the world like this."

"I know that."

"When?"

"Soon, I hope," Masuto told her. "I have just a few questions that might help. For one thing, did your ex-husband own a pistol?"

"Yes."

"Do you know what kind?"

"I'm afraid not. To me, one pistol is the same as another."

"Did you ever see it?"

"Yes."

"Well, you do know what an automatic pistol looks like and how it differs from a revolver. Was his an automatic pistol or a revolver?"

"I think it was an automatic pistol. I'm not sure."

"And by any chance did he belong to the same pistol club that Alan Greene belonged to?"

"Yes, I think he did."

"Thank you," Masuto said. "I'll only ask you to endure this through the rest of this evening. One way or another, it will come to an end."

"I hope you're right," Beckman said as Masuto was leaving.

"We're trying."

Masuto got into his car, but instead of driving off, he sat there brooding. He was a meticulous man; that came with his Japanese ancestry and with his Zen training. His Zen training had taught him how elusive the truth is and it had also enabled him to use his insight to capture flashes of the truth. The meticulous quality went along with his distrust of his flashes of insight.

He released the hood of the car, got out, raised the hood, and stared at the motor. He had never wired a car with dynamite, yet faced with the necessity he felt he could pull it off. Six sticks of dynamite in a confined spot behind the engine, a detonator stuck in place with so simple a device as a couple of Band-Aids, and then a lead from the ignition.

He closed the hood of his car and sat down behind the wheel. Again he brooded for a while. Then he called the station on his radiophone. "Put me through to the captain," he told Polly.

"For a dashing, handsome Zen Buddhist Oriental, you are the most unromantic person I know."

"The captain, Polly."

"What's up?" Wainwright asked.

"I'm troubled and I'm nervous."

"Maybe you ought to knock it off. Go home. Give it tomorrow."

"That's no good. If I let this go until tomorrow, something will happen tonight. I feel it in my bones."

"You got the three dames boxed up with Beckman.

If you want me to go over there and lecture them, I will. I'll talk them into staying put another night."

"That won't do it. He's too aggressive, too bold. He's running for his life now."

"Well, damn it, Masao, what do you want me to do?"

"I want to pick him up."

"Are you crazy?" Wainwright exploded. "Maybe you got another career lined up, but I got twenty years in this police force. What are you going to charge him with? Picking his nose in public? You got nothing on him, nothing but that crazy intuition of yours. I believe you because I know you and I seen this happen before, but you got nothing. Bring me something. Bring me the gun, and we'll pick him up in a minute."

"It wouldn't help. He's using Billy Fuller's gun."

"What the hell does that mean?"

"It means that Fuller's gun was stolen."

"Did he report it?"

"He only discovered the theft today."

"And what makes you so sure our man stole it?"

"I'm not. Just another guess. You can be sure the gun will turn up, and then when the bullets are matched, it leads straight to Fuller."

"And it's also a beautiful alibi for Fuller."

"Yes, it works both ways. You won't pick him up then?"

"Masao, we can't. All we'll have is one beautiful lawsuit, and if he hits the city for a million bucks, we can pack up and go."

"All right."

"Where are you off to now?"

"Maybe to find the missing piece."

Masuto started his car and pulled out of the driveway. It was only about a mile to Tony Cooper's hairdressing establishment on Camden Drive. It was past six o'clock, and the streets of the business section were empty. Masuto wondered whether he had delayed too long.

He parked his car in front of the beauty shop, and through the glass window, it appeared to be a repeat of the night before. Cooper stood over a single customer, combing and shaping a head of black hair. He glanced at Masuto as the detective entered, raising an eyebrow. Masuto nodded, took a seat at the side of the room, and then sat silently and thoughtfully, watching Cooper. Cooper, he decided, was quick, skilled, and meticulous. He recognized the quality. Whatever Cooper did, he decided, he would do well. Why then had he come to hairdressing? Why does any man come to what he gives his life to? Why had Masao Masuto become a policeman?

Questions were easier than answers. The woman whose hair was being cut had fingernails as long as a Mandarin's; they were painted bright red. They were claws on the ends of her long fingers, and above the hands, the wrists were encased in jeweled bracelets.

Cooper finished. The woman signed the pad he held out to her. Masuto wondered what the monthly bill of a woman who used Tony Cooper's hairdressing shop amounted to.

Cooper took her to the door, and then closed and locked the door behind her. "Do you wait until you see me with my last customer?" he asked Masuto.

"Just a coincidence."

He dropped into the chair next to Masuto and stretched out his legs. "Have you caught your killer yet?"

"I'm close."

"But not close enough."

"That's right. Not close enough. It's like putting a jigsaw puzzle together. You solve the puzzle, and then when you've finished, you discover that two or three pieces are missing."

"I noticed you were looking at that woman's fingernails," Cooper said.

"You notice things. That's a rare gift."

"To a great many men, those long, painted red fingernails are pretty disgusting. I've had men tell me it's a complete turnoff. Yet the women do it. I guess they feel it's a sex symbol."

"Or a class symbol. You don't mop floors or play a piano with those fingernails," Masuto said. "You know, the missing pieces can be the most important."

"Missing pieces?"

"There's no time left," Masuto said. "There's no time to play games. Anyway, I don't like to play games. Not when someone's life is at stake."

"Don't you tend to dramatize, Sergeant?"

"Now look," Masuto said, "don't be deceived by the fact that I don't act the role of a TV cop. I'm not joking and I'm not playing games. I told you yesterday that I didn't give a damn whether you were a homosexual or not. I don't. But if you keep on lying to me, I'll make you wish you were never born. I'll slap more violations on you than you can carry. I'll hound you right out of this town, and don't think I'm making empty threats. So if you want me to walk out of here and forget that we ever met, just answer my questions and answer them truthfully."

"You got one hell of a nerve! You can't come in here—"

"I can and I am! Now why didn't you tell me that Mitzie Fuller worked here?"

"You didn't ask me." He took a deep breath. "Anyway, she was only here a week and she only worked mornings."

"Did the other women know her then?"

"No. That was before they became my customers."

"Why did she leave?"

Cooper hesitated, and Masuto said, "I want it all. All—and quickly."

"Because I wanted to marry her."

"You're gay."

"And what you don't know about gay, Mr. Detective, would fill a book. Sure I'm gay. That doesn't mean I can't fall in love with a woman. That doesn't mean I can't stop being gay."

"But she didn't marry you?"

"She would have. She just said that she saw too much of that kind of marriage end up as tragedy. She didn't want to do it to me or to herself."

"So she married Billy Fuller."

"Yes."

"They were married six months. What broke up that marriage after six months?"

"Why don't you ask Mitzie? Why don't you ask Fuller?"

"You know damn well that I asked them and that I got nowhere."

"Maybe that's the way it should be. Maybe there are some things that even cops don't have the right to know."

"Granted. I'm not curious, Cooper, and I'm not peddling gossip. I could guess the answer to the question I asked you, but it's no damn use for me to guess. I have to know."

Cooper sat with his legs stretched out, staring at his clasped hands. The moments ticked by. Finally he said, "You really think this creep intends to kill those dames?"

"Yes, I do."

"Mitzie?"

"Yes, Mitzie."

"Okay. Here it is. Mitzie was a hooker, a hundred-dollar-a-night hooker. Billy Fuller married her without knowing that. Can you imagine what it did to a man with Fuller's phony macho when he found out? I'm amazed he didn't try to kill her right then and there. Oh, he slapped her around all right. She showed me bruises the size of purple plums. But mostly he cried. Mitzie said if the little bastard weren't so impossibly nasty, she would have felt sorry for him. That after he used her for a punching bag."

"How did he find out?"

"You always got a good friend who'll tell you what you don't have to know."

"But when she was married to him, she had stopped?"

"Hooking? Yes, of course."

"I'm not up on all the folkways. Now exactly when did she begin to work as a prostitute?"

"Is that important?"

"Yes, very."

"Mitzie is twenty-nine. She came to Los Angeles about eight years ago, dreaming the old impossible dream. And it is impossible, believe me. She worked around as a waitress, and that's when I got to know her, maybe six years ago when she was waiting a joint around the corner. I talked her into a job here, because I wanted her around and because I thought she was the prettiest kid I ever saw. Well, she was already turning a trick every now and then, and after she left here, she didn't go back to slinging hash."

"She became a full-time prostitute."

"If you want to call it that."

"What would you call it?"

"I don't call it. To me, it's no worse than being a cop."

"We won't discuss that. You said she was a hundred-dollar-a-night girl. You don't walk the streets and pick up hundred-dollar customers. Did she have a pimp?"

"No!" Cooper snapped. "She hated their guts."

"Then how did she work?"

"Do you know a place called The Bar?"

"Just that, The Bar?"

"That's right. It's in Hollywood, up on a hill to the left as you drive into Laurel Canyon. A driveway up to a parking lot, and then from the parking lot up a staircase. It's got a lot of color and a wonderful view of the city lights. It's a bar and restaurant, and the food isn't bad, and it's the kind of place people go when they don't want to be seen. There's always two or three girls working out of the place, and the guy who runs it, George Denton, is pretty decent to the girls. It brings him trade. There's no cheap pickup. I suppose you could call George a pimp, because if a guy wanted something, George hustled it, but he never took more than ten percent from the girls. Mitzie worked out of that place until she met Fuller. I guess she met him two years ago. He gave her a couple of small parts, but she was no great shakes as an actress."

"And that's it?"

"That's it."

Masuto rose and held out his hand. "Thanks, Cooper."

Cooper took his hand. "Forgive me for not getting up. I'm washed out. I work my ass off in this place, and I don't know for what."

Masuto let himself out, closing the door behind him.

A strange world, Masuto thought, wherein he earned his daily bread, a world of sunshine and palm trees and million-dollar mansions where a girl with the face of an angel was a hooker and a Zen Buddhist was a cop and a grocery store in Beverly Hills sold tomatoes for a dollar and seventy cents a pound and a boutique sold dresses that weighed less than a pound for three thousand dollars. But, he wondered as he got into his car, was any world less strange? On a planet gone mad and apparently intent upon destroying itself, was Beverly Hills abnormal?

He maintained his sanity and his equanimity by refraining from judgments. He did his work, and although it was past quitting time, he still had work to do.

He drove north to Santa Monica Boulevard and then to Sunset Boulevard, through the Strip into Laurel Canyon Boulevard. Somewhere in back of his mind was a recollection of a place called The Bar. It went back through the years, but the more he plucked at it, the more it eluded him.

There on his left was the modest sign and the arrow. THE BAR. He turned onto the driveway and drove up to the parking lot, a high angle drive about a hundred yards long. Half a dozen cars were already there. Against the wall of the hill, a wooden staircase went up another forty feet or so.

Masuto climbed the staircase. From the landing at the top, the view was magnificent, the whole of the Los Angeles bowl spread out in front of him, glittering in the night like some vast jewel. He was never unconscious of the beauty of Los Angeles. The beauty resisted the most fervent march of tackiness and bad taste that the development, which is euphemistically called civilization, had ever produced. The beauty fought back, even, as Masuto thought in his more optimistic moments, as truth and decency fought back.

He looked at the view for a moment or two more, and then he went inside. Like most Los Angeles restaurants, the place was underlit. Lamps on the tables, a few lights at the entrance, but for the most part a muted interior. There was a bar, a screen, and a dozen tables. At the far end, a spinet piano at which a black man inprovised the blues.

A tall, good-looking man of about fifty, dark-haired, with a long, narrow face that had become habitually fixed in an expressionless mask, wearing working evening clothes, approached Masuto. He studied the detective, examining his battered tweed jacket, his wrinkled gray flannel trousers, and his tieless shirt.

"Can I help you?" The noncommittal question which left a variety of outs.

Masuto showed his badge.

"Would you come into the light?"

Obligingly, Masuto put the wallet which contained his badge under the reservation light. "Detective Sergeant Masuto," he said. "Beverly Hills police."

"Aren't you out of your territory, Sergeant?"

"Mr.—"

"George Denton."

"I see. This is your place?"

"That's right."

"Now I'm sure," Masuto said, "that you know enough about the way the law functions in Los Angeles County to know that I can go anywhere in the county in pursuit."

"Is that what you're doing?" Denton asked sardonically. "Hot pursuit? Isn't that what the law says?"

"That's what I'm doing."

"Well, look around you. I know every customer in the place. No criminals. So unless you got a warrant, I'd rather not have the fuzz around. It gives my place a bad name."

"Your place has a bad name."

"What are you talking about?"

"Just this," Masuto said quietly. "You're running a classy whorehouse. Now I don't mind you defending your business, but don't knock mine. I'm a mild-mannered person, but I've had a long day, and I'd just as soon come down on you like a ton of bricks as not. I don't owe you one damn thing, and if you think I couldn't smash this joint and close up your lousy business, just try me. And if you think I'm off my own turf, I'll pick up that phone and have two black-and-whites here in five minutes, and then you can tell your story to the L.A. cops."

"Hey, wait a minute. Hold on."

"And you'll address me as Sergeant Masuto."

"Okay, Sergeant. Okay. Look, I run a quiet, decent place here. No one gets cheated and no one gets rolled. I been in business twelve years and I never had no trouble. You can't blame me for getting a little riled when a Beverly Hills investigator comes in and starts asking questions. My God, why would you want to close me up? I'll show you places in Beverly

Hills with five times the action we ever have here."

"I don't want to close you up. I want some information."

"Okay, Sure. Come over here and sit down." He led Masuto to a small table near the bar. "Can I get you something to drink?"

"No, thank you. Do you know Mitzie Fuller?"

"She was Mitzie Kogan when I knew her. That was before she married Billy Fuller. I suppose he found out that she had turned a few tricks, and that finished their marriage. She was a good kid. A real beauty. A real strawberry blonde beauty. But she hasn't been back here since she met Fuller. She told me she wasn't coming back. I was glad. I wished her luck."

"That was how long ago?"

"Almost two years ago."

"And before that, how long did Mitzie work out of this place?"

"Three years, give or take a few months."

"How did it work?" Masuto asked. "I mean, what time did she turn up?"

"Between eight and nine most of the time. You can see, there's not much action before then. Of course, there were nights when she'd come in at six or seven and just hang around listening to Joe over there playing the piano. She was crazy about his blues, and you don't hear much blues these days, nothing but rock."

"Joe was working here then?"

"That's right. I keep my help. That ought to say something about the kind of a place I run."

"Would Mitzie stand at the bar or sit at a table?"

"Sometimes the bar, sometimes a table, sometimes up there with Joe. It would depend. Say, what's she into? I'd hate to see that kid get hurt."

"So would I." Masuto took a picture out of his pocket. "Do you know this man?"

"I know him," Denton said, studying the picture. "His name was Smith, but that ain't his name. Nobody's name is Smith."

"Do you know his real name?"

"No. I'm not curious about the customer's names."

"When did he first come here? Can you remember?"

"Jesus—who can remember? Maybe four years ago, maybe a little more. He gave Mitzie a short fling. Then he turned up with a girl, and after that, no more Mitzie. Mitzie left him alone. Like she never saw him."

"He came back with the girl—or was that the last time?"

"He came back, two or three times a week. Why not? My food is as good as anything in L.A. and the prices are not out of line. I don't bother people and I don't ask questions."

"Didn't he use a credit card?"

"No, cash. Always cash. That's all right. This is a place where men come with other men's wives. It happens. I handle a lot of cash."

"Always with the same girl?"

"Yeah."

"And how long did that go on?" Masuto asked.

"Maybe nine months."

"And what did he call the girl? And what did she call him? If they were here that many times, you must have heard names."

"Yeah. She called him Jack and he called her Kate."

Masuto took out of his pocket the picture of Kelly—Catherine—Addison that Beckman had lifted from the album in Laura Crombie's bedroom. He put it in front of Denton.

"That's the girl."

"You're sure?"

"Of course I'm sure."

He put the picture back in his pocket. "What was their relationship?" he asked Denton.

"What do you mean?"

"You know what I mean. You watched them night after night. Were they sleeping with each other?"

Denton shrugged. "I'd say so. I don't know what the kid saw in him, except that he was good-looking and knew his way around. These stupid kids go for older men. I didn't like him. I felt he was a bastard. So did Mitzie. But what the hell, it was no business of mine."

"Can I talk to Joe?" Masuto asked, nodding at the black pianist.

"Yeah."

"How's his memory?"

"Better than mine."

He took Masuto over to the black pianist. "Joe, this is Sergeant Masuto of the Beverly Hills police."

Joe nodded and went on playing. "A Nisei. They're beginning to integrate."

"Talk to him."

"I'm not crazy for fuzz," Joe said.

"I said, talk to him."

"Okay, boss. I'll talk." He stopped playing. Masuto took out the two pictures. Joe nodded. "That's right. That's the poor kid who went off the road up on Mulholland. Her name was Catherine Addison. You remember," he said to Denton, "I told you about that."

Denton didn't remember. He wasn't covering,

Masuto decided, he just hadn't remembered. He remembered now.

"I'm sorry, Sergeant," he said.

"He don't read the papers. I do," Joe said. "I think I told him but I'm not sure."

"Was she here the night she died?" Masuto asked him.

The black man closed his eyes and with one finger began to pick out a mournful tune on the piano. Masuto waited. Denton turned away to deal with a customer.

"Yes," Joe finally said.

"And the man?"

"Yes."

"Were they happy?"

"What's happy, Sarge? Who's happy? No, they was not happy. The kid was crying. She came to me and asked me to play 'Blues in the Night.' I ain't crazy for it, but I played it."

"Was Mitzie here that night?"

The black man's eyes turned cold, as if he had pulled a film over them. "I don't know nothing about Mitzie."

"I like Mitzie," Masuto said. "I'm trying to save her life. Maybe what you tell me could save her life. That's the truth."

He thought about it for a while, his finger picking out a tune again. Then he said, "Yeah, Mitzie was here. Mitzie came over to me and asked me if I knew why the kid was crying. I remember because we never saw her again. We never saw Smith either."

"You wouldn't remember what time that was?"

"Jesus, man, you want a lot, don't you? That was over three years ago. All right, I can tell you this. It was before the tables began to fill, so maybe it was before eight o'clock."

"Thanks, Joe," Masuto said.

"No sweat. Only don't make it hard for George. He's a decent man."

Chapter 14

THE KILLER

"Am I going to have trouble?" George Denton asked Masuto.

"Not unless you make it for yourself. I'm not a vice cop. Now I have to use a telephone."

"Sure—sure, Sergeant. Use this one right here."

Masuto dialed Laura Crombie's number. It was busy. He dialed it again. Busy. He was becoming increasingly nervous, increasingly irritated. Couples were coming into the restaurant now, an occasional single woman, an occasional single man. The women were good-looking, the men well-dressed, middle-aged. An open menu told him that the least expensive entrée was twelve dollars.

He dialed again. Beckman answered. "Masao— thank God! We been turning the town upside down for you."

"What happened?"

"Mitzie's gone."

Masuto controlled an impulse to explode with anger. "All right," he said evenly. "Tell me exactly what happened, short and quick."

"She got a call from someone said he was Wainwright, and he said he was calling for you, and she was to meet you."

"Where?"

"I don't know. All the ladies know is that it was a bar."

"God damn you, where the hell were you?" Masuto demanded.

"In the can, taking a crap."

"Oh, great—in the can!"

"There are times when you got to."

"And you called Wainwright and it wasn't Wainwright."

"Right. Jesus, Masao, who would think of it? She saw a chance to get sprung and she shot out of here in that yellow Porsche of hers. We got out an All Points. What do I do now?"

"Don't let either of those women out of your sight, if you have to tie them up. Wait a minute. What did she say—a bar or the bar?"

"Hold on."

Masuto heard Beckman calling out to the women, "What did Mitzie say—a bar or the bar?"

And then in the phone, "Masao, they think she said The Bar."

"All right. Tell Wainwright to put everything he has on that yellow Porsche."

Masuto slammed down the phone and bolted out of the door of the restaurant. Below him, he saw the yellow Porsche pull into the parking lot. A man stood there. As the yellow car stopped, the man opened the right-hand door and got in. Masuto was already racing down the stairs, three at a time, as the Porsche pulled out of the parking lot.

Masuto took the last six steps in a single bound, ran to his car, started the motor, and then found the narrow driveway blocked by an incoming car. He waited, cursing himself for being a fool, for not having a second man in the house with Beckman, for not seeing the whole pattern and anticipating what would happen—and most terribly for a death that he could have prevented.

The driveway was clear, and he shot down it to the Laurel Canyon intersection. The Porsche was nowhere in sight. He had two choices. He could turn right down into the city of Los Angeles, and if the Porsche had gone that way, it was hopeless even to dream of finding it. That might be the clever turn for the Porsche if the man knew he was being followed. But there was no reason for him to suspect that he was being followed. On the other hand, if Masuto turned left, the road led up to Mulholland Drive, and in the past there was a connection with Mulholland Drive.

Masuto turned left. He threw his car into low gear, gunning it ahead and almost crashed his way into the line of traffic that was crawling up the single lane of Laurel Canyon Boulevard. He could hear the curses of the drivers, but he was unwilling to put on his siren and announce the chase. If he did and if the yellow Porsche was ahead of him, it could leave his Datsun as if his car was standing still. Instead he took risks that no sane man would take, swinging into the left lane again and again to pass cars, forcing oncoming cars to squeeze over to the wall of the canyon, bulling his way back into the traffic again and again.

As he approached the top of Laurel Canyon Pass, where Mulholland Drive intersects it, and where Laurel Canyon Boulevard sweeps on down into the San Fernando Valley, another choice faced him. If indeed the yellow Porsche was ahead of him, it had three choices: to continue ahead and down into the Valley, to turn right and follow Mulholland Drive to Cahuenga Pass, or to turn left on Mulholland. Since he couldn't see the car he hoped he was following, if indeed he was following it, he could toss a mental coin. Except that it was not in Masuto's manner to toss coins for lives, even mental coins. Just as he himself was in violent motion, so, he believed, was the killer. The killer would do what he had done twice before, turn left and westward on Mulholland Drive and let the road be the murderer.

Masuto saw the traffic light at the top of the pass now, red, with a line of cars stopped in front of it. He pulled into the left-hand lane, providentially empty, and roared up to the top of the hill, taking a left turn on two wheels and then racing down Mulholland Drive, his headlights cutting a crazy twisting beam through the night.

It was, Masuto remembered, one mile and seven-twentieths, as Officer Commager had read it from his report. It was not history repeating itself, but the tortured, maniacal mind of a sick man. There was a limit to how fast any car could go on this road. Masuto pressed his car to that limit, screaming around the curves, with the whole sparkling spread of the San Fernando Valley a thousand feet below him, with his tires skidding almost to the edge of the sheer drops that lined the road.

And then he saw it in front of him, the yellow Porsche, the motor hood in back of the car open, and the man, standing there bent over the motor, and then straightening up to see the car approaching. At that point on the road, there was a shoulder of earth off the right lane. A car could park there while the traffic went by—yet there was almost no traffic on Mulholland at this hour—and that was where the Porsche stood, off the road, its nose facing the edge of the cliff.

Masuto's brakes screamed and his tires skidded as he headed straight for the Porsche. Then the man had a gun in his hand, and he began to fire at the oncoming car. It all happened in the space of a second or two, the man standing and shooting, three holes in the windshield, the bullets so close that Masuto could almost feel them as he ducked down behind the wheel, and then the scream of a black-and-white's siren. Masuto opened his car door and propelled himself out, skinning his hands on the road, rolled over, pulling out his gun—and then saw the man who had fired at him leap over the edge of the parking place into the black, mesquite-covered hillside.

The black-and-white pulled up alongside his car, and two Los Angeles cops leaped out, covering him with their drawn guns.

"Just drop that gun, mister, nice and easy."

Masuto let his gun drop.

"Are you that crazy bastard who just drove up Laurel Canyon?" the other cop asked. "Because if you are, we are going to throw everything the book says at you."

"I'm Detective Sergeant Masuto of the Beverly Hills police. There's a girl in that car who needs attention, if she's still alive. So call an ambulance."

"Just don't move, mister."

The other went to the Porsche. "Get an ambulance, Joe."

"Is she alive?" Masuto wanted to know.

"She has a pulse. She has a bad crack on the head, but she's alive. Who did you say you are?"

"Masuto, Beverly Hills police. If you'll let me put my hand in my pocket, I'll show you my badge."

"All right, but nice and slow. I got a nervous finger."

Masuto took out his badge and handed it to him. While he was studying it, the other officer looked at the Datsun.

"Three bullet holes in the windshield. What in hell goes on here?"

The officer called Joe was handling Masuto's gun, smelling it. "Not fired," he said.

The other cop gave Masuto's badge back to him.

"Let me look at the girl," Masuto said.

"Better not move her."

"Where's the guy who did the shooting?"

The door of the Porsche was open. Mitzie was slumped behind the wheel, a huge welt on the side of her head. She stirred and groaned.

"I asked you, where is the guy who did the shooting?"

Masuto pointed down the dark, mesquite-covered hillside. "He went down there."

"Then that's where we ought to be looking."

"In the dark? Forget about that," Masuto said.

"You're pushing a lot of weight around here for a Beverly Hills cop."

Now a second black-and-white pulled up, and with it, the ambulance. Sergeant Jack Kelly, in the second black-and-white, knew Masuto.

"Thank God for a friendly face. Kelly, will you tell these guys that I'm legitimate? They almost shot me."

"What goes on here?" Kelly asked.

"A damn lot," Masuto said. "Down there"—pointing over the edge "—is a man who's wanted for three killings in L.A. and for a fourth in Beverly Hills. The woman they're putting in the ambulance is the witness who's going to hang him. If you talk to Pete Bones downtown, he'll fill you in. But what's important now is that no one gets near that woman. Her name is Mitzie Fuller—"

"Hold on, Masuto. If that son of a bitch is down there, we ought to be down there looking for him."

"In the dark? He's half a mile away by now. There's a whole ring of houses around the canyon. All he has to do is pick up a car and get out, and maybe by now he's done that. Don't worry about him. I know where to find him. The important thing is the girl. Hold up there!" Masuto called out to the ambulance driver. And to Kelly, "I'm going with the ambulance. The keys to my car are in the ignition. Can you have someone drive it over to the Beverly Hills station on Rexford?"

"What about the Porsche?"

"Are the keys in it?"

Kelly looked. "They're there."

"Send them both to the station, and give the keys to whoever's on duty. I'm going to steer the ambulance to All Saints in Beverly Hills."

In the ambulance, Mitzie Fuller opened her eyes and began to cry. She tried to talk. Masuto put his finger across his lips. "Later, Mitzie, later."

"I want to tell you—" she managed.

"I know. There's nothing to tell me. Don't try to talk."

"She'll be all right," the attendant said. "She wouldn't be talking like that if it were anything worse than a bad concussion."

"I hope so," Masuto said, and then dropping his voice, "you might get an inquiry. Any inquiry. Just say you took her to All Saints in Beverly Hills."

"You don't want it kept quiet?"

"No."

Mitzie was trying to talk again. "He wanted to kill me—"

"I know, Mitzie. The danger's over. I want you to rest."

It was almost ten o'clock when they reached the hospital. Mitzie Fuller was taken into the emergency room. Masuto went to admissions, where Sister Claridge was on duty.

Sister Claridge managed to squeeze a smile out of her long dour face. "What now, Sergeant? What awful things do you bring us tonight?"

"It's the nature of my work, Sister. We brought a lady into emergency. Her name is Mitzie Fuller, and she has a concussion. In other words, someone hit her over the head and tried to kill her."

"It just gets worse, doesn't it, Sergeant? Worse and worse."

"Perhaps. Or perhaps it's always been this way. The point is this: I want her put in a room, but I want the records to show her in another room. In other words, when inquiries come, I want whoever it is directed to the second room."

"Why?"

"Because someone may try to finish the job, and I'll be in the room he comes to. I don't want her there."

"Isn't that rather dramatic, Sergeant?"

"It comes with being a cop."

"We'll bill her for the room she's in. We'll have to bill the police department for the other room."

"Just for me to sit there?"

"Hospital rules. You're using the room. We'll have to change the linen." The smile was gone. Sister Claridge considered Masuto an unredeemed heathen. For a time she had tried, gently, to show him the path. Lately, she had given up. "Also, Sergeant, I'll have to check with my supervisor. We can't have violence here in the hospital."

"I'm trying to prevent violence, Sister. Now what room can you give me?"

Still she hesitated.

"I'm trying to save her life—and the lives of two other women. Please help me," Masuto said quietly.

She sighed and nodded. "All right. Room three fifty-one."

"Thank you. And spread the word, please. Hospital people, floor people, and anyone who calls, friends, press, anyone. Room three fifty-one."

"I feel like a conspirator," the sister said.

"In a good cause. Is there a phone I could use?"

She pointed to a booth on the main floor. Masuto looked longingly at the phone on her desk. She shook her head. "I'm sorry. It's for hospital use only. Really, Sergeant, you can't walk in here and use the hospital as a police station."

He went to the booth and called Wainwright. Mrs. Wainwright answered the phone in a tone not unlike that of Sister Claridge. "He is not here, Sergeant," she said acidly. "He's at the station."

Masuto called the station. Wainwright's snarl was almost comforting after talking to the two women.

"Where the hell are you?" Wainwright demanded. "The whole thing busts loose, and you disappear. Do you know that Mitzie Fuller's gone? Beckman let her walk out of there. I'm going to have his head for this—"

"Take it easy. Beckman couldn't help it."

"Why? Because he was taking a crap? Who the hell says he has to take a crap when he's on duty! If that dame's dead, we can all spend our time on the crapper."

"She's not dead."

"How do you know?"

"Because she's here with me at All Saints Hospital. She got a nasty concussion, but she's all right."

"Why am I always the last to know? What happened?"

Masuto summed it up as tersely as possible.

"You can't be sure that he'll try it tonight," Wainwright said.

"It's in his nature. He's in motion, and now he's desperate. He planned this whole thing like a lunatic chess game, and it came to pieces at the seams. That girl's testimony will send him to the gas chamber."

"For what, Masao? For attempted murder. You still have no way to tie him into the murders."

"Mitzie can."

"You tell that to the D.A. when the time comes."

"I have the owner of the bar and the piano player."

"To do what? To tell us that he was there?"

"Captain, don't worry it. Let me pick him up. We have the assault on the girl and the shots he fired at me. If the bullets are in the car, we may have something. And he'll have a gun tonight."

"Which gun? You don't think he's walking around with the murder weapon?"

"I'll talk to you later," Masuto said.

He came out of the booth and walked over to Sister Claridge. She nodded smugly. "I trust I'm doing the Lord's work and not the devil's work, Sergeant Masuto. While you were in the booth, a gentleman called. He said he was Mrs. Fuller's husband."

"Mrs. Fuller is divorced."

"I am simply telling you what he said. He said he was Mrs. Fuller's husband. He was very concerned about her condition. I told him she would be all right but we were keeping her here overnight. He was very insistent on seeing her tonight, and I told him at this hour it would be impossible. I told him we were discharging her at ten o'clock tomorrow morning and that he could pick her up then."

"Did he ask what room she was in?"

"Yes, he did. And I told him she was in room three fifty-one."

"Thank you," Masuto said. "You did nobly. I don't know how he'll get in, but if anyone comes through the front door between now and midnight, I want you to pretend to be dozing. For your own safety."

"That's ridiculous!"

"Please, please do as I say. I don't have the time to stand here and convince you. All the odds are that he won't come in the front door, but if he does—"

"I don't know why I'm going along with this—"

Masuto went to the elevator. On the third floor, he said to the nurse on duty, "I'm Sergeant Masuto, Beverly Hills police. I'll be in room three fifty-one. You can check that with Sister Claridge. If a man comes up here and asks for Mrs. Fuller or for room three fifty-one, don't stop him. If anyone—doctor, attendant—if anyone wishes to go into room three fifty-one, don't interfere."

"But—"

"No buts," Masuto said harshly. "I don't have the time. And if anyone asks, I'm not in that room. Mrs. Fuller is—alone. Do you understand me? And above all, do not interfere."

Then Masuto walked down the corridor and into room three fifty-one. It was a very ordinary hospital room, one window, the hospital bed and two chairs. There were two pillows on the bed. On a shelf in the closet, Masuto found a third pillow and two extra blankets. With the pillows and the blankets, he put together a vaguely lifelike form which he covered with the counterpane, pressing it into shape. Then he switched on a small blue night light and switched off the overhead lights.

Then he went into the room's bathroom and stood there in the dark, his gun in his hand, the door open just a crack. His mind was clear, without memory or anticipation. He was aware of himself, of his feet on the floor, of the gun in his hand, and of his view of the room through the crack in the door.

Nothing else existed. Time did not exist. When finally he heard the steps outside the door, he had no notion of how long he had been waiting there. The door opened. The man stepped into the room, grotesque in the blue light. For a long moment, the man stood without moving, one hand in the pocket of his jacket. Then the hand came out with the gun, the heavy, long-nosed .22-caliber automatic target pistol. The gun came up, and he fired into the bedclothes, five shots, one after another, lacing across the simulated body.

Masuto kicked the toilet door open and snapped, "Drop it, Crombie!"

Crombie was very quick. Masuto lived because he was in the dark, because he presented no visible target, but Crombie got off two more shots before Masuto fired. Crombie's shots splintered the edge of the bathroom door. Masuto's single shot caught Crombie between the eyes.

Chapter 15

THE QUESTION

It was after one o'clock in the morning when Masuto drove his Datsun, three bullet holes in the windshield, into the driveway of Laura Crombie's house on Beverly Drive, parked, and rang the doorbell. They were still awake, and a tired, harassed, and miserable Detective Beckman answered the bell and opened the door.

"I don't know what to say, Masao," he pleaded. "I never goofed off like that before."

"Forget it. Maybe it was the only way. At least it's over."

"That's what we heard," Beckman said.

"I want to talk to Laura Crombie."

"They're both in the kitchen drinking coffee."

He led Masuto into the kitchen. Nancy Legett poured a cup of coffee for him. Laura Crombie sat at the end of the table, her face gray and tired.

"How is Mitzie?" Nancy asked.

"She's all right. She'll be out of the hospital tomorrow."

"And I can go home?"

"You can go home."

"Sit down and drink the coffee," Laura Crombie said. "You look as terrible as I feel. Do you want some cookies?"

"No, thank you."

"Beckman says it's over."

"It's over."

"Beckman says it was Arthur. I don't understand that," she said. "What possible reason could Arthur have for wanting me dead?"

"He didn't want you dead. He wanted Mitzie Fuller dead."

"Why?"

"I'm going to tell you about that, Mrs. Crombie. If I don't tell you, you'll hear anyway, in dribs and drabs, with all the innuendo that the newspapers and the media can make of it. That's why I came here tonight—to tell you the whole story very precisely. It's going to be very painful, but there's no way to avoid that. Sometime about four years ago, maybe a few months more, your ex-husband, Arthur Crombie, met your daughter. She fell in love with Crombie."

"No!"

"You must listen to me," Masuto said, almost severely. "I can't spare you. You must know the truth. As I said, she fell in love with Crombie and they had an affair. Then Crombie met you. I don't know where he met you, but it was in circumstances apart from your daughter."

"Yes," she whispered. "I met him at Acapulco. Then I went to Boston. He was here. Kelly was here—oh, my God."

"He decided to marry you. But to do this, he had to dispose of Kelly. There was a place where they met, called The Bar, a restaurant off Laurel Canyon. He met her there one night. They drove off to Mulholland Drive in her car. He hit her as he had hit Mitzie, and then he wired the throttle of her car to take it over the cliff."

Laura Crombie was weeping now. "That's enough. I can't stand any more of this. I can't."

"You can and you will," Masuto said coldly. "There are no more secrets. Do you want to read about it tomorrow?"

"Please, must you?" Nancy Legett begged him.

"Yes, I must. Now listen, both of you. That last night he was in the restaurant with your daughter, people had seen them together. Mitzie was there. She knew who he was. The others didn't. But Mitzie did not know who the girl was. She did not know that Catherine Addison was your daughter, and she had no reason to think that what had happened on Mulholland Drive was anything but an accident. Three years went by, and then you brought Mitzie into your bridge game, and Arthur Crombie learned about it. If you're in the real estate business in Beverly Hills, there's very little you don't hear about. He realized that sooner or later Mitzie would see a picture of your daughter—and that would open up the whole can of worms. So he hired a chemist with a criminal record, paid him to prepare a batch of poisoned pastry and deliver it here. He didn't care how many of you died—as long as Mitzie died. The rest of you were a diversion to cast suspicion elsewhere, as was the box of poisoned candy he sent to Alice Greene. Then he killed Alice Greene, to throw suspicion on her husband. He killed the chemist to keep his mouth closed. He killed a Chicano boy for the same reason. And finally, tonight, he tried to kill Mitzie Fuller. There was nothing human left in this man, nothing to shed a tear over. He had become a monster. Now he's dead."

Masuto stood up. "Drive Mrs. Legett home, Sy. As for you, Mrs. Crombie, I'm sorry it had to be this way, but that's the way it is. You're safe enough now. It's over."

At the door, as Masuto was leaving, Beckman said to him, "You were pretty hard on her, Masao."

"Was I? Don't you think it's time she faced up to reality? She's lived with illusions all her life, the illusion that the whole world's like Beverly Hills, the illusion that a human pig can be a decent man, the illusion that you buy happiness—ah, the hell with it!" And he went out, slamming the door behind him.

He got into his car and drove back to Culver City. The light was on in the kitchen, and he entered the house by the side door. It was two o'clock in the morning. Kati, wrapped in a kimono, was waiting for him. She stared at him, and then she cried out, "Oh, Masao! What happened?"

He managed to smile. "Indeed? What happened to your raised consciousness? I thought you would be furious. I forgot even to telephone you."

"I called Captain Wainwright. Oh, I was upset, but when you walked in, your face was so sad, so very sad."

"I killed a man, Kati."

"Oh, no."

"An evil man—but, Kati, I am not one to judge and I judged him."

Being a wise woman, she deflected his thoughts. "I have hot soup on the stove, very tasty. I am sure you had no supper. And while you eat, I'll draw a hot bath."

"That would be so good, a hot bath."

After his bath, he dried himself and slipped into his saffron robe.

"You're not going to sleep now?"

"I can't sleep."

"What will you do?"

"I'll meditate for a while."

"And then you'll sleep?"

"I'm sure."

"Then I'll go to bed. I can sleep as long as you're home. Masao—?"

"Yes?"

"I know you don't want to talk about it, but this evil man—what did he do?"

"He murdered five people—"

"No, you must not talk about it," Kati said.

Masuto went into the sun parlor, which he liked to think of as his meditation room. It was cold here, but that was good. It would help him to stay awake. He sat down cross-legged and tried to make his mind empty and calm. But he could not erase Wainwright's words from his mind. They had no evidence to convict Crombie of the murders. He was convinced that when they examined the bullets tomorrow, they would not match the bullets used in the murders. For those, Crombie had used Fuller's stolen gun. The chemist was dead and the Chicano boy was dead. Had he, Masuto, known that there was not enough evidence to convict Crombie of the murders? In the fraction of the second, when Crombie was shooting at him, had he come to a decision to be both judge and jury? Could he have wounded Crombie and taken him alive? His shoulder was a better target than his head.

But as much as he asked himself the question, he was unable to come up with an answer. The gray light of dawn was in the sky before his mind stilled itself and he had stopped asking the question and was finally able to meditate.

Dell Bestsellers